What Readers and Reviewers Are Saying

"This book does an excellent job of explaining the process of training guide-dog puppies, a topic that will fascinate many children . . . the moving scenario will have readers sniffling as Diego passes Aloha's leash to Miss Kimberly Louise, and may even lead them to consult the appended list of resources to find out about raising their own guide-dog puppies."

—School Library Journal

"*Hello, Goodbye, I Love You* is a lovely and charming account of what it is like to raise a guide dog puppy and the bittersweet emotions associated with loving them and then letting go. I know your book will touch many hearts and inspire young adults to reach out in their communities."

—Lori Mogan, Public Affairs—Guide Dogs for the Blind, San Rafael, CA

"What a fantastic book! It is well written with excellent pacing and makes a fascinating story. Ms. Bauer Mueller truly paints a poignant portrait of the love that goes into training one of those special needs dogs."

—Georgeanne Irvine, Author, Public Affairs-San Diego Zoo

"*Hello, Goodbye, I Love You* depicts a love journey between a puppy raiser, a guide puppy's training and a visually impaired woman, and how they become one. There are many guide dog programs, as noted by the author. From my experience as a past District Governor of Lions Club International, I can attest that the same love journey occurs many times yearly in each guide dog school. "

—*Patrick J. Pignataro, Past Lions Club District Governor, GA*

"The sweetness of this book comes through on every page. Pamela Bauer Mueller has hit all the right notes in a story that informs as well as entertains."

—*Cary Knapp, Columnist/Librarian, Brunswick, GA*

"*Hello, Goodbye, I Love You* is a wonderful book. The story is captivating with intricate details making it funny, sweet, heart tugging, and precious. From the day Diego receives Aloha to the end of the story you are truly touched. Your eyes will be opened to the amazing miracles dogs can be for the trainer as well as for the recipient of the guide dog."

—*Virginia Belt, Brunswick, GA, 14 years old*

"A wonderfully told, tender story about a young Mexican boy who trains a guide dog for the blind, and discovers that his life has changed forever.

—*Suzi Hassel, Educator, Brunswick, GA*

"What a sweet and moving book. It accurately represents

the joy and pain of raising a guide dog puppy. The book should come with a warning that you will need tissues to soak up the tears of joy!"

—Richard Sadowsky, Guide Puppy Raiser, Beaverton, OR

"When Diego's mother reminded him that his puppy was on loan to him from God, and that raising her was a gift of service to others and a privilege, but not his to keep, I realized that this book was very impacting to children as well as informative to those training the dogs for the blind. I greatly enjoyed this book and would definitely recommend it to others."

—Jane Fiebick, Elementary School Educator, Bend, Oregon

"Aloha will work her way into the hearts of her readers just as she does with Diego and his family. Diego and his friend, Jeremy, knowtheir guide dog puppies are only 'on loan' to them while they prepare the puppies as companions for sight-impaired people. Little do they know how it will end . . . This is a heartwarming story about boys, friendship, and seeing the world through different eyes. Anyone considering raising a guide puppy will find the book very helpful as well as enjoyable. Research has made the story an accurate portrayal of a guide puppy's first year."

—Bette Dennerline, Librarian,
Highland Park Middle School, Beaverton OR

Also by Pamela Bauer Mueller

The Kiska Trilogy

The Bumpedy Road

Rain City Cats

Eight Paws to Georgia

Hello, Goodbye, I Love You

The Story of Aloha
A Guide Dog for the Blind

PAMELA BAUER MUELLER

PIÑATA PUBLISHING

Piñata Publishing
112 Dunbarton Drive
St. Simons Island, GA 31522
912-638-2676

www.kiskalore.com

CANADIAN CATALOGUING IN PUBLICATION DATA

Mueller, Pamela Bauer
Hello, goodbye, i love you: the story of Aloha, a guide dog for the blind / Pamela Bauer Mueller.

ISBN: 0-9685097-3-8

1. Guide dogs—Juvenile fiction. I. Title.
PZ7.B324 HE 2003 J813'.54 C2003-910069-3

Cover design by Annie Krebs

Typeset by Vancouver Desktop Publishing Centre
Printed and bound in Canada by Ray Hignell Services Inc.

This book is dedicated to all the selfless guide dog raisers,
the marvelous guide dogs, and to their valiant
sight-impaired partners everywhere.
You have my greatest admiration.

and

In loving memory of Naomi Marie Weiler,
the most brilliant star in the sky.
August 9, 1979-December 7, 2001

Acknowledgments

I need to thank many people for helping me get this material together. I am indebted for assistance, advice and research support to the following people:

Tommy Jenkins, who led me to Lions Club International and the Georgia Lions Camp for the Blind;

Shannon Nettles, Camp Director at Georgia Lions Camp for the Blind in Waycross, Georgia, who provided the assistance of her staff and campers for my research;

Annie Krebs, my artistic friend and cover designer, whose cheerful disposition and numerous talents made working with her a pleasure.

Ticiana and Ted Gordillo, for advice, editing, encouragement and loving support. Thank you for bringing Aloha into my life!

Cassandra Coveney, for your gracious offer to edit my book and your precise counsel.

Virginia Belt and Marcie Hunter: my first manuscript readers. You gave me the valuable youthful insight that I needed.

John Belt, my young buddy, who helped me learn the "lingo" of twelve-year-old boys.

Louise Hooper and Kim Belt, whose friendship inspired the character "Kimberly Louise." Thank you for reading my manuscript, offering insightful changes, and cheering me on!

My Reunion Group, "The Gals of Grace," for loving me and lifting me up. Thanks, Julie, Tyler, Kim, and Louise.

Pamela Pollack, my "book doctor," for your guidance, expertise and creative suggestions.

Sharon Castlen (Integrated Marketing), my friend and guide, for your insights, sweet encouragement and for making work fun!

And particular thanks to:

Cary Leach, Joanne Ritter and Lori Mogan from Guide Dogs for the Blind, for the many hours and inexhaustible energy spent helping me make the manuscript accurate and educational.

Michael Hingson, thank you for writing the heartfelt Foreward to the book, and for giving your amazing expertise to the guide dog program.

As always, I thank my fabulous publishing team: Patty Osborne, the bookmaker, and Ray Hignell, the printer. You are both brilliant and clever; always helpful.

A very special thanks to my beloved husband, Michael, for his constant support and invaluable help in bringing the manuscript through its various lives. And thank you for making delicious dinners while I wrote!

Aloha, thank you for being the awesome dog you are and for giving me a glimpse of the possibilities.

Finally, I wish to thank my dear friends, who will find themselves deftly disguised and meandering throughout the manuscript. Each one of you is often in my thoughts.

Foreword

You are about to experience a joyous treasure in *Hello, Goodbye, I Love You*. Pamela Bauer Mueller has painted a wonderful and true picture of the raising and early training of a guide dog by Diego, an American boy of Mexican descent with a dream. Diego, Aloha, Kimberly Louise, and all the characters in this book bring out the best in all of us. They show why America is the land where many cultures and species can work together to make our world a better place. I am the recipient of the gifts of characters like those in this book. Let me explain.

It has been 38 years since I received my first guide dog Squire from Guide Dogs for the Blind. I still remember the day.

It was a Wednesday afternoon in July of 1964. My instructor, Mr. Bruce Benzler, called me into the instructor's office and asked me to sit quietly in a chair. I heard Mr. Benzler open a door and call Squire into the room.

Squire entered and then, as dogs do, began to sniff around. Quickly, however, he must have seen me for he stopped investigating the room and came straight to me. He began sniffing me all over.

After some thirty seconds of examination by Squire, Mr. Benzler said, "It looks like you have found a friend."

I had indeed found a friend for life. I was fourteen when I met Squire. He stayed by my side as my guide and companion for nine years. He went through high school, college, and my first year of graduate work before retiring to live with my parents. I still have the degree Squire received when I graduated from the University of California at Irvine in 1972. Chancellor Dan Aldrich called Squire to the podium to present a special degree to him in front of the entire class and viewing audience. I will always have a special place in my heart for Squire. I grew up with him. I learned more from Squire than I have time to tell. Working with him helped teach me to be a more responsible person.

Looking back, I can see that Squire's raiser, Nancy

Nichols, a student and member of a 4-H club, did a tremendous job of raising him. It must have been hard for her to give him up so he could go on to his advanced studies and then to being my guide and friend.

I know it was hard for Nancy because it was hard for me to decide to retire Squire nine years later. Making those hard decisions is part of what we, raisers and users alike, learn from these loving and wonderful dogs. The puppy raising staff and trainers of Guide Dogs for the Blind can't make easier our decisions to return puppies or retire dogs, but they do help us to understand the importance of moving on. The Guide Dogs' staff is always there to help, guide and comfort everyone involved.

After Squire, I have had the joy to know four more guide dogs from Guide Dogs for the Blind. I also got to meet each dog's puppy raiser. Each dog gave me more than I can ever repay. Every guide dog was a success because of the selfless devotion, love, and dedication of the puppy raiser.

To me, the most dramatic example of the successful raising and training of a guide dog took place on September 11, 2001. My fifth guide dog, Roselle, and I were in our office on the 78th floor of Tower One of the World Trade Center in New York, when the tower was deliberately struck by an airplane as part of the worst terrorist attack in history. Roselle and I descended the stairs to escape from the burning tower.

Later, we ran for our lives when the second tower collapsed less than a hundred yards from us.

Roselle and I lived that day because of our fabulous close bond. The work of two incredible people, Kay and Ted Stern, made it possible for me to meet and bond with Roselle. The Sterns raised Roselle for Guide Dogs for the Blind. I have come to know them well since I received Roselle in December of 1999. Kay and Ted helped Roselle grow into a well-balanced and confident guide. They took her everywhere they traveled. For me, the Sterns' work with Roselle was as much a gift from God as Roselle herself.

Of course, nothing could totally prepare us for 9-11. However, the Sterns, their puppy raising leaders, and the Guide Dogs for the Blind puppy raising staff did the work that provided me with the angel who helped me run away from a collapsing 110-story building. I know that without Roselle's guidance and friendship on 9-11, I would not be here today to write these words.

Since 9-11, 2001 I have come to know much more about the process of raising and training guide dogs. I joined the staff of Guide Dogs for the Blind in February 2002. I chose to move to California to this wonderful school to give back some of what I have received over the past 38 years. I now travel throughout the world speaking to companies and organizations on a variety of topics including, of course, guide dogs, puppy raising, and the wonderful life-long bond we develop with our furry partners. My speaking fees go directly to Guide Dogs for the Blind to further the grand work it has been doing for the past sixty years.

If you want to learn more about being a puppy raiser, please visit the Guide Dogs for the Blind website at http://www.guidedogs.com. If you are blind and want to learn more about guide dogs or would like to submit an application to receive a guide dog, you may do so at the same web site. If you are blind, going blind, or if you have a family member or friend who is blind, I hope you will learn from this book that life goes on after someone loses his or her sight. Blindness is not the tragedy many believe it to be. As blind people, our biggest handicap is not the blindness. Rather, the handicap is the perception others and we have about blindness. We use alternative techniques to live, work, get around, and do everything else that sighted persons do.

Living life is what it's all about. Whether blind from birth, or becoming blind from a loss of sight later on, we each need to make the choice as to whether to live life to the fullest or not. Many like me have found that guide dogs are great teachers as well as unconditional givers.

Dr. Jacobus tenBroek, founder and first president of the National Federation of the Blind, spoke in 1956 of William

Bradford, who in the 1600's spoke that now famous phrase: "There but for the grace of God go I." I, like Dr. tenBroek, prefer to say, "There within the grace of God do go I".

If after reading this book you think about raising a guide dog puppy, I urge you to explore it. You will have fun. Young or old, you will learn something. You will make new friends, dog and human alike. Finally, you will be involving yourself in a tremendously rewarding and worthwhile effort.

I hope you will enjoy what you are about to read. This book is a real picture of the process of raising a guide dog puppy. There is not much more worthwhile than performing the job of guide dog puppy raiser.

Diego and Kimberly Louise, we applaud you and thank you for teaching us all. Aloha, thank you most of all for the work you do. You and those like you have brought so much joy, friendship and guidance to so many of us, blind and sighted alike. Please keep up the good work.

Michael Hingson
National Public Affairs Representative
Guide Dogs for the Blind

Prologue

Diego took a deep breath and closed his eyes, fighting to keep the tears from slipping out. *I knew this day was coming,* he told himself. *Why can't I stop thinking about losing her?* He stole a quick glance at Aloha, sitting quietly by his side and waiting for his command.

Any minute now, girl. Help me get through the speech and not mess up. Aloha, could you please give me some of your courage? he pleaded softly.

Aloha turned her face toward Diego as if she understood his thoughts. Her rich chocolate eyes smiled up at him and her tail thumped softly. *She knows,* thought Diego. *This day is a victory for her, but she is confused by my sadness. I've got to pull myself together for Aloha and her new life.*

Then Diego heard his name called from the podium. He pulled back lightly on the leash. "Aloha, let's go," he directed. Together they climbed the stairs and walked to center stage. Diego looked into the audience and quickly found his family. Smiling shyly, he felt his courage returning. Before he began to speak, he bent over and lifted Aloha's chin up so their eyes met. "Thank you, Aloha," he whispered tenderly. "I'm letting you go now, but always remember how much I love you."

Chapter One

When spider webs unite, they can tie up a tiger.

—Ethiopian Proverb

The puppies were truly beautiful. Not even three weeks old, they were fat and roly-poly and already pushing their way around their mother and each other in the wading pool where they were born. The little one they called Aloha was the noisiest and most playful of them all. She snuffled and groaned and hurled herself across their living quarters. She was not the largest of the five, but was most definitely the leader.

None of the puppies had to be bottle fed because their mother Maggie was strong and healthy and had enough milk for them all. Maggie was hand picked four years ago for this purpose, and had never let them down. She was one of the selected stock dogs to breed in the whelping kennel in San Rafael, California.

Maggie had been brought to the whelping kennel ten days before her puppies were due. She surprised them all by having her litter four days early and birthing five healthy pups. Her puppies were born in a stall inside a plastic wading pool, lined with newspapers and heated by radiant heating coils. This kept them all warm and cozy.

Now they were preparing to move them to the floor of the kennel and give them solid food. They would not be totally weaned from Maggie until they were six weeks old. Closer to their six-week birthday, each pup would be given a name and receive a permanent tattoo in both ears. These tattoos were made with a green vegetable dye and represented an identification the dogs would carry throughout their lives.

George and Rosalie Anderson had offered their home to breeding female Labradors seven years ago, and Maggie was the latest of their female stars. She was a sweet-tempered sleek yellow Labrador Retriever. They loved her and decided to keep her after her breeding days were finished.

Rosalie and George were delighted with each of the new yellow puppies, but the smallest was by far their favorite. She was very light colored, almost white, with a dark line across her nose, which resembled the bridge on a pair of eyeglasses. They named her first and called her Aloha, after fond memories of their Hawaiian trip. When they researched Hawaiian words, they learned that "aloha" means, "Hello, Goodbye, I Love You." What a perfect name for the little one!

Next they named her brothers and sisters, deciding on Alma, Annie, Attica and Aztec. All littermates are given names that start with the same letter of the alphabet. These names would be submitted to the puppy raising department at Guide Dogs for the Blind and quite possibly would be accepted.

After they were six weeks old, the Andersons were able to visit Maggie and her puppies on a regular basis, getting to know each member of the litter during their first eight weeks of life.

"George, I think these are the most beautiful puppies I've ever seen," gushed Rosalie.

"Dear, you say that every time our dogs have puppies," he answered.

"No I don't. Look at how frisky and bouncy they are. Did you see how Aloha wrinkles up her nose in a little smile? And look at Aztec and Annie falling over their clumsy feet!"

The Andersons were always saddened when the pups were moved away to the puppy kennel, but they were happy to have Maggie return to their home. This usually happened shortly after the puppies were seven or eight weeks old. George and Rosalie paid them a final visit to kiss them good-bye and wish them well. They never chose to accompany the puppies to the kennel because it made them too sad.

When the five squirming puppies arrived at the puppy kennel on campus, several volunteers carried them to a large stall, where they were immediately fed. The volunteers later walked them and introduced them to the outside world.

Guide Dogs for the Blind has campuses in San Rafael, California and Boring, Oregon. Maggie's new litter would be going to Boring, Oregon. Volunteers from the San Rafael campus worked with the puppies, helping them discover and accept strange noises, new smells and situations that were previously unknown to them. They learned to overcome their initial fear of surprises and loud noises.

The volunteers adored all of the puppies they cared for. They helped them get used to their names by playing with these wagging, wriggling, licking pups whenever they could. The puppies also enjoyed their interaction with each other, and quickly learned to wrestle, play tag and hide-and-seek, and defend themselves from each other's nips and bites. The world must have seemed perfect to Aloha and her littermates!

Chapter Two

Hold a true friend with both your hands.

—Nigerian Proverb

Diego Escobár opened his eyes and felt very happy. His last dream before awakening was about Guadalajara, Mexico. It was a great dream because he had just returned from a two-week visit with his cousins in Guadalajara. He smiled as he realized that his Mamá would be pleased that he was thinking and speaking in Spanish in his dream.

In three weeks he would be entering the seventh grade and he would no longer be in the youngest class in his middle school. Although his whole summer vacation had been awesome, Diego liked school and was excited to be returning. As great as the summer had been, he knew today was going to be the best day of his life! He was getting a new puppy! Not just an ordinary puppy, but a yellow Labrador Retriever. And he would be raising this very special puppy for Guide Dogs for the Blind!

Diego jumped out of bed and moved quickly through his room. He felt impatient and wanted the morning to hurry into afternoon. They couldn't leave for the Guide Dogs for the Blind campus until 3 o'clock. Of course, he could fill up the time with his chores, or maybe even finish the library book he was reading. But he was too excited and nervous to concentrate on reading.

"I know," he said out loud. "I'll call Jeremy and see if he's got everything ready for his dog. Then we can go pick them up together."

Jeremy Hunter was Diego's best friend, and luckily they were both getting a guide dog on the same day. They were physically opposite in appearance and temperament. While Diego had a thick head of curly brown hair and dark eyes, Jeremy had straight medium length blond hair and green eyes. Diego was shy and soft-spoken; Jeremy was outgoing and clever, always the center of attention. The boys had known each other for eight years, and they were inseparable.

The boys lived in Beaverton, Oregon, an attractive and pleasant suburb of Portland. They enjoyed Beaverton's rolling hills, lush forests, rivers and abundant parks. Because life was calmer there and less hectic than in the city, young families were drawn to Beaverton to pursue goals and raise families. Diego's family had moved there from California when he was only three years old. Diego loved to recall the story his parents shared about how they met.

Both his mother and father had left Guadalajara, Mexico when they were teenagers and immigrated to Los Angeles to work in the fields alongside their parents. After working just one summer, their parents realized that an education would be their greatest asset, and sent Maria Teresa and Ernesto to school. While getting an education, they realized they had fallen in love. They chose to marry in Mexico, surrounded by family and friends. When they returned to California, they vowed to speak Spanish together and later teach it to their children.

Maria Teresa and Ernesto Escobár did teach their children Spanish from childhood, but as Diego grew older and brought friends to his home, he asked his parents to speak to him in English. It seemed rude to Diego that his friends could not understand what he and his family were saying. His parents agreed, continuing to speak Spanish to each other, knowing that the children would one day be grateful.

Diego rushed downstairs into the kitchen and ran into his mother as she carried plates to the table. "Mamá!" he exclaimed. "Can we ride up to Boring with Jeremy and his parents? We can bring back both of the puppies in one car!"

"That sounds like a great idea," she answered with a smile. "Let's see what Jeremy's folks say."

Sometimes Diego felt a little different from his classmates because of his Mexican heritage, yet he was thankful that his parents were passing on the Mexican traditions to his younger sister Clara and him. He beamed at his mother as he realized how proud he was of their ambitions and accomplishments. His father had worked his way up from packer to manager of a local Beaverton clothing store. His mother worked as a part-time court translator, utilizing her Spanish in such an important position.

Diego suddenly realized he was daydreaming. There were plans to make and no time to waste. But before he could make that phone call to Jeremy, his mother called him to the table for breakfast. He waited impatiently while the others finished so he could be excused. Finally, after sending his nine-year-old sister some intimidating looks, Clara picked up her fork and finished her waffles. He jumped up from the table and ran to the phone.

"Hey Jeremy, my Mom says it's okay if we all go together to pick up our dogs! Do you guys want to ride with us in the van? We'd all fit fine and then the puppies can ride together one more time before we have to separate them," he suggested excitedly.

"Cool. Let me ask my Dad."

The boys arranged to meet at Jeremy's at 2:45 that afternoon. All four parents and Clara would make the hour trip to the campus in Boring to pick up the puppies. Everything was going so well today. Diego could hardly wait until the afternoon. He just knew that this was going to be the greatest day of his life!

Chapter Three

Everyone in his own house, and God in all of them.

—Cervantes

Kimberly Louise Walker loved living in the south. She even liked summertime in the south, with the feel of humidity against her skin and the heat and stickiness in the air. Just when she thought she couldn't bear to be outside, the tender winds would blow through the ancient oak trees, swaying the trailing Spanish moss and rustling the marsh grasses below. Whenever she traveled to other parts of the world, she missed the gentle heat and longed for her beautiful little coastal island.

She walked through her elegant living room and stopped to check herself in the mirror. Her walk had always been athletic: an aggressive stride that announced her approach. Time had softened it into a feminine sway that complimented her. Her auburn hair was swept up and twisted behind her head, accented by a pair of ivory chopsticks. She wore pearls at her throat and ears. Her startling sapphire blue eyes were both wise and youthful, twinkling with a light of warmth and humor. She smiled at her reflection and strolled out to the sun porch.

Kimberly Louise hadn't always lived on St. Simons Island. She was born in Savannah, Georgia, where she was brought up to be a proper young lady. When the time came to choose a college, Kimberly Louise decided to go to the other side of the country. Her cousin from Spokane, Washington was attending a small liberal arts school in Portland, Oregon: Lewis and Clark College. Kimberly Louise convinced her parents to let her visit the college, and after spending two days there, she fell in love with the Pacific Northwest. Four years later she received her Bachelor of Arts in education, and shortly after that, her Masters degree.

But the call of the marshlands was powerful, and Kimberly Louise yearned to return to Georgia to teach. She applied to and was accepted at a high school in Savannah, where she taught for ten years. During this time, Kimberly Louise married Larry Walker and had two children, Julia and John Henry. The family then moved to Atlanta, Georgia and spent the next fifteen years enjoying the bustling city life.

Her children grew up and moved away, starting careers and later, families of their own. Kimberly Louise and Larry made a surprising move to New York City to accommodate his career in journalism. For eight years they thrived in and enjoyed New York. Yet she often dreamed of returning to the south. Sadly, her dream came true, but only after Larry lost his battle with cancer.

One of Kimberly Louise's dear friends in New York City had a winter home on St. Simons Island, Georgia. Shortly after Larry's death, the two women went to the island and stayed at the beach cottage for three months. Kimberly Louise was enchanted by the dignity of the ancient moss-laden oak trees. She took great pleasure in the late afternoons at the beach, when the sky was broad with lights of pink and orange, and the sun's bright ball began to fade. She realized she had to live there, and two months later she moved to the island. She enjoyed surrounding herself with the beauty of lush foliage and the magnificent magnolia, oak and cypress trees.

On this late summer afternoon she was swinging in her rocker on the porch, drinking sweet tea and watching the squirrels noisily scrambling up the thick trunks of the live oak trees. Her friends would soon be by to pick her up and take her to play bridge on nearby Jekyll Island. As she rocked back and forth on her deep veranda that wrapped around both sides of her house, she could feel the temperature dropping slightly as the white clouds scurried across the sky. They were quickly replaced by darker clouds casting long black shadows. Several moments later the raindrops began, lazily at first and then picking up in intensity.

"Oh dear," she muttered, "I think we're in for a storm. I'd better go get my raincoat and umbrella before they arrive.

Looks like this beautiful day is changing into something else."

At that moment she could not possibly know the changes that were about to affect her life.

Chapter Four

Friendship is a single soul dwelling in two bodies.

—Aristotle

Diego looked over all the puppy raisers and their families who were gathered in the Visitors' Center at Guide Dogs for the Blind's campus. He noticed that there was only one other kid raising a puppy besides Jeremy and himself. She said her name was Wendy and she was thirteen. She quickly informed the boys that she knew all about raising puppies. She declared that this would be her second puppy to raise. The other puppy raisers were adults of all ages; there were more than twenty people waiting to receive their dogs.

"Diego, when will they bring them out?" muttered Jeremy as they were being given last minute instructions on caring for their pups. "This is killing me. I want my dog now!"

Diego did not want to appear impolite by talking while they were being instructed.

"Jeremy, shhh!" he whispered, trying to concentrate on the program.

They had already received pamphlets, the raiser's manual, and lots of reading material during the three months they had been meeting with their Puppy Raiser Club leader. So they felt like they knew what was expected of them. The puppies were waiting for them in their kennels.

"And now comes the moment you've all been waiting for." The instructor interrupted Diego's thoughts and brought him back to reality. "As we call your name, please follow us and we will take you to your puppy. Your family can accompany you, and from there, you will be taking your puppy home."

At last! Diego, Jeremy and Wendy all exchanged nervous, tentative smiles and waited for their turns. The instructors knew that the two boys were riding together, so they were among the first to be called. Diego's heart was pounding loudly as he walked with his parents and Clara to the kennels. He knew he had never been this joyous, or this certain about accepting any responsibility.

"It's so cool that we get to do this, Jeremy."

Clara's brown eyes were wide with anticipation as she approached the kennel, her father's hand in hers.

"Do you think our puppies already know each other?" inquired Jeremy.

They all spotted the two frisky light yellow Labrador

puppies at the same time. The pups were wriggling and rolling and nipping at each other. Diego felt goose bumps all over.

What incredibly beautiful puppies! He just couldn't stop staring at them. And to know that one of them was his!

"Diego, meet Aloha," the instructor said with a broad smile. "She is so happy to meet you."

Diego looked down at the little dog with a dark mark over her nose, who was busily licking the other puppy's face. He was thinking that this adorable puppy looked like she had sunglasses on. As he turned to share this thought with his family, Aloha sat down.

She looked up at him, staring directly into his eyes. She watched him for a moment, then wrinkled her little nose in a smile and thumped her tail with pleasure. After a few seconds, she calmly sniffed his foot and leg and lay down beside him.

Diego was mesmerized. He eagerly reached down to pick her up. "Hello Aloha," he whispered into her ear. "I know you and I are going to be very happy together!"

Chapter Five

Dark is a long way.

—Dylan Thomas

As they left St. Simons Island and crossed over the Torras Causeway, Kimberly Louise remarked that the rain was coming down unusually hard. Silver dollar sized drops spattered on the windshield, making it difficult for her friend David to drive and see clearly. He turned the wipers up to high and suddenly realized he was struggling to control the car. He wondered if the women had noticed. Just then a gust of wind blew them towards the road's shoulder.

"Hold on, everyone," he joked good-naturedly. "I think this storm was sent to keep me from winning all your money in bridge. Do you want to stop and wait it out?"

Mimi leaned forward from the back seat. "David, you get us to that game so I can reclaim all the money you took from me last week! Just go slowly and we'll be fine."

At that moment, Kimberly Louise felt a ripple of fear

coursing through her. Turning to David, she noticed that his brow was furrowed in deep creases. "David, I would feel better if you pulled over and parked on the shoulder," she said quietly.

They waited out the rain for about ten minutes. It ended as quickly as it had started. The sky began to clear and the dark clouds were breaking up. David eased back onto the highway and everyone breathed a sigh of relief. As they turned off the highway to enter Jekyll Island, Kimberly Louise noticed the heavy tension in her neck and shoulders and tried to relax. She closed her eyes and rotated her shoulders, breathing deeply. She could feel the tightness flowing out of her body.

Her peace of mind was abruptly shattered.

"David!" screamed Mimi as her hand flew forward and clutched his arm. "Look out!"

A large black jeep from the opposite lane was spinning around toward their side of the road. They could see the cars ahead of them veering to the right to avoid the ill-fated jeep. David was squeezing and rotating the steering wheel, desperately trying to keep them out of the path of the oncoming vehicle. As Kimberly Louise looked on in disbelief, the jeep grew larger in her vision. It slid and spun wildly toward them. Her hands flew to her mouth and her eyes fixed in horror on the jeep looming before the windshield.

"Oh, dear Lord," she moaned, just before the explosion of light and sound. She felt sweet thick blackness flooding through her, burying her deep and warm within herself.

Chapter Six

No one gets far unless he accomplishes
the impossible at least once a day.

—Elbert Hubbard

Diego watched Aloha sleeping soundly in her crate next to his bed. It amazed him that she was so content and adaptable. Only fifteen days ago she had left her littermates to live with him and had not cried for them at all. He thought how fortunate he was that she was able to spend most of the day with him since school had not yet started. And what a lucky break for him and Jeremy that Aloha and his dog, Alma, were sisters!

Diego had joined the local 4-H Club last year partly so that he could work on team projects and learn to feel comfortable interacting with others. He didn't like being shy and hoped the 4-H Club would help him overcome it.

"Papá, were you afraid to give speeches to your class when you were in school?" he asked Ernesto one evening.

"Yes, I was, because I stuttered when I was a young boy," his father answered.

"How did you get over it? You don't stutter now," Diego added.

"Well, I often made up short stories for my younger brothers and sisters, and one day a teacher asked me to write them down. Then I read them to my class, and other teachers asked me to read them to their groups. Soon I realized that I became so comfortable with my stories that I gained self-confidence and stopped stuttering."

"Wow! I don't stutter but I have a hard time talking to groups, too. I guess I just think that I don't have anything important to say."

"Confidence takes time, *mi hijo* (my son)." Ernesto put his arm around Diego's shoulder.

One evening at a 4-H Club meeting Diego heard about the Puppy Raiser Program at Guide Dogs for the Blind. After the meeting, he raced to Jeremy's house on his bike.

"Jeremy, don't you want to get a dog?" he asked breathlessly. "Here's a way our parents will let us have one. We raise them for a year or more, and we probably will even get to take them to school with us. How cool is that?" Diego was excitedly explaining the program to his best friend.

"Way to go, Diego! Let's do it! We'd be the only ones in our school with dogs!" Jeremy wanted in on all the excitement.

Both families had agreed to the boys' requests to raise a

guide dog puppy. Jeremy readily glowed in the attention their puppies were causing. Diego was beginning to feel comfortable with the questions asked by total strangers.

"Can I pet your dog?" asked a little boy in the mall as they were walking by his table.

"Yes, but I'll get her to sit first," said Diego with a smile. "Aloha, sit."

Aloha immediately sat down and looked up to Diego for approval. "Good girl." He rewarded her with a pat on the head and then invited the boy to pet her on her shoulders.

"She's such a good puppy," beamed the boy. "And she looks so cute in her coat." Diego knew she looked adorable in her green and white "Guide Dog Puppy in Training" jacket.

Later that afternoon, Diego and Jeremy took their puppies on a long walk through a quiet park in Beaverton, Oregon. The tall hemlock and Douglas fir trees offered shade to the tired quartet. They relaxed beside a brook and skipped rocks across it, while the puppies rested and observed.

Diego felt so happy, and knew that his best friend was equally thrilled with Alma. It was great having littermates, living close by, and being able to compare their daily accomplishments and antics.

"Aloha follows me everywhere," he bragged to Jeremy. "She wants to jump on the chair when I sit down, but I make her stay on the floor like they told us."

"Dude, Alma cried the first few nights when we kenneled

her, but now she's used to the crate and loves sleeping next to my bed," replied Jeremy with a smile.

"Aloha doesn't wake me up too early to do her business like she used to. What about Alma?" asked Diego.

"Sometimes she whines a little by my bed, but I just tell her 'later' and she goes back to sleep," laughed Jeremy.

Both boys were very involved in training their puppies to "do their business," which was the terminology they learned from the raiser manual to toilet train them. The dogs were taught to do their business on command, and were fed and given water accordingly. This meant the boys had to wake up early and take the pups outside around 5 a.m. for the first break, and then feed them their breakfast. About every two hours for the rest of the day they took the little Labs outside on leash and issued the command to do their business. Sometimes they had to wait for the dogs to finish, but they always rewarded them with lots of praise and enthusiastic vocal rewards.

"Aloha, you sure are curious," Diego told the little puppy as she pulled on the leash to smell just one more boulder. "Aren't you ready to go back home and take a nap?"

Hearing her name, Aloha sat down at his side and tilted her head, searching his face expectantly. Diego wondered if she understood the words "home" and "nap." He was proud of how quickly she was learning, and knew his puppy would be a bright leader dog.

"*Vámanos, muchachita linda* (let's go, beautiful little girl)," he cooed to her. Grinning broadly when he realized he was speaking to her in endearing Spanish words, he started for home. Jeremy and Alma got up to follow them. Each boy was delighted with his good luck.

Chapter Seven

"For I know the plans I have for you," declares the Lord,
"plans to prosper you and not to harm you,
plans to give you hope and a future."
—Jeremiah 29:11

Kimberly Louise threw back her head and laughed. She held Tyler's little hand and ran with her to the ocean's edge, enjoying the soft breeze blowing through her light auburn hair.

"Sweetie, you beat me!" she praised her granddaughter as they dropped to their knees in the shallow water. The small waves at East Beach were no threat to them and they completely immersed themselves in the warm water.

"Nana, you let me win. You are bigger so you can run faster." Tyler was a precocious and bright child, whose every thought and word delighted Kimberly Louise.

Tyler's older brother Jonathan was calling to them to join him in deeper waters where he was boogie boarding with friends. Kimberly Louise smiled and waved to him, then closed her eyes and listened to her granddaughter shriek with delight as she drifted and bobbed among the waves.

She enjoyed the island all year round, but especially loved the summertime when her grandchildren visited. Jonathan was already eight and little Tyler would soon be five. How time seemed to fly these days! Her daughter Julia and her husband Donald spent last week with them on the island, and then agreed to leave the children for another week with their grandmother when they returned home. This was the first time Kimberly Louise had been able to convince them to do this. Floating on her back, she smiled at this great blessing. As she watched her precious grandchildren sharing the natural beauty of the area with her, she basked in the emotions of happiness and peace.

Kimberly Louise struggled to open her eyes. The pain kept tugging at her. She eased away, retreating until she felt the blackness return. She let images of the past float through her, directing all thinking inward. Everything was moving so slowly, and she fought to stay buried deep within herself. She felt like her eyelids were stuck together. She tried prying them open with her hands and realized her hands were secured to the bed.

If this is a nightmare, she thought, *please let me wake up soon.*

She wanted to stay buried, but felt herself returning to the room. She fought her mounting panic and took some long, deep cleansing yoga breaths. With effort, she slowly forced her eyes open, but a dark veil seemed to cover everything in her path. Then she saw only white.

"*Where am I?*" she wondered.

A shot of pain coursed through the back of her head, and she welcomed the warm darkness that pulled her back into a deep and senseless sleep.

Chapter Eight

Gratitude is a memory of the heart.

—J.B. Massieu

"Hurry up, Clara, or we'll be late for the meeting," called Diego from the doorway.

"Mamá, I can't find my scrunchy," wailed Clara. She was in a terrible mood.

"You go on, honey. I'll find it later," replied Maria Teresa.

Diego was annoyed with his parents for letting Clara attend the Puppy Raisers' meeting with him when she was only nine years old. How could she possibly help train Aloha? Immediately he realized he was being unfair. Clara was already helping him out on walks and feedings, and she was so pleased when he or his parents complimented her on her good work. He put an arm around her shoulder, picked up her rain hat and placed it on top of her dark curls. Now they were ready to go.

Jeremy was waiting in the car with his father and Alma. The puppies had been with them for over a month now, and were quickly learning the commands. The raisers had been teaching their dogs several commands, and so far their dogs had begun learning "forward," "sit," "down," "do your business" and "come." They were still working on the command "stay."

Their school had agreed to let them take the dogs for three days a week. The other two days Aloha would stay home with Maria Teresa, or accompany her to work when she translated in the courthouse. Alma would keep Jeremy's mother company the days she didn't go to school with him.

Diego and Jeremy enjoyed rewarding their puppies with both verbal praise and the physical praise of petting, stroking, and especially hugging. They were taught that treats or the promise of a toy were unacceptable rewards, and were delighted to see their little Labs respond happily to the approved rewards. On the other hand, the raisers had to learn how to correct inappropriate behavior. Both boys understood that the only acceptable corrections were leash and collar corrections, and the dogs were learning these rapidly. A quick tug on the leash showed the puppy that a certain behavior was inappropriate. Then the boys showed the pup how to do it correctly.

There was so much to learn. Diego had some problems with Aloha's barking, which she tended to do when she was excited or there was another dog in the area. He was correcting this with the leash and collar, but needed the guidance of other raisers. Thank goodness for the Puppy Raiser meetings!

As they entered Jeremy's car, Aloha twitched her ears, raised her eyebrows and gave Alma a lick on the nose. These two puppies seemed to know that they were sisters, and always celebrated their meetings with affectionate gestures.

Today's meeting was held in a school gymnasium. There were thirteen puppies and about twenty raisers and family members present, in addition to Nancy, the club leader. Happily, Clara found her girlfriend Hannah who was helping her older sister raise a Golden Retriever pup. She sat with them and left Diego with his group of friends.

The group discussed puppy-training techniques. Nancy explained again that through consistency the puppy would learn that his reward would arrive quickly, but only after he completed the task.

"Remember guys," she repeated. "Our motto is Fairness, Patience, Persistence and Consistency."

Each raiser was given an opportunity to bring up particular problems and questions.

Elena, a sixteen-year-old immigrant from Russia, complained that her German Shepherd puppy was not displaying good manners around her cats and parents.

"He seems distracted when we're all together," she complained. "He gets annoyed and excited and seems really nervous with so much stimulation."

"Aztec loves to jump up on the sofa," interrupted Wendy. "We're having such a hard time correcting him."

"You must leash and collar correct him, Wendy," offered Nancy. "And then give him lots of praise when he returns all four feet to the floor. Elena, maybe you need to keep Shadow's distraction level lower until he becomes used to more people and especially to your cats."

Each raiser was guided through his or her particular problem, and Diego found it fascinating to hear all the behavioral and socialization dilemmas. He secretly felt that Aloha was far beyond the other puppies, but then reminded himself that each raiser probably shared his feelings about their dogs.

"Alma barks when cars stop in front of our house, and she growls when someone rings our doorbell," reported Jeremy.

As Nancy discussed the correction techniques, she brought up the subject of puppy trading for eventual overnights or over the weekend visits. She explained that the puppies should do visits in someone else's home about once every quarter during their stay with the raisers. Diego didn't want anyone else to care for Aloha, not even for a weekend. But he kept his opinions to himself, too shy to speak up but hoping that someone else would.

"Do we have to give our puppies to another raiser for an overnight?" asked Elena. "I really think Shadow will get more confused with someone else correcting him."

Nancy explained how important it was for the puppies to pay attention to and obey someone other than the raiser. All the puppies needed to learn to socialize, particularly with other raisers.

Diego again noticed that both Aztec and Alma were larger than Aloha. He had been told that she was the smallest of the litter, but seeing her next to them emphasized the difference. She was also the lightest in color, almost white, and certainly the only one with the dark "eyeglass bridge" mark over her nose. He and Jeremy called the mark her sunglasses look. Secretly, Diego loved it that she was unique.

The afternoon wore on with the many questions and stories. Once again, Diego realized that he had no complaints regarding Aloha's behavior. She did like to chew on things, but seemed to understand what was okay to chew and what was not. The raising program allowed her to chew on certain toys, and that seemed to satisfy her.

"I wonder how the other littermates are doing," said Jeremy to Diego. "It's too bad that they are in other areas of Portland and don't attend our club meetings. How can we contact them to find out?"

At today's meeting two of the attendees played instruments, which were new to the dogs' ears. One raiser played a guitar and was accompanied by a flute. Diego noticed that Aloha and Alma seemed to enjoy the music.

He nudged Jeremy. "Look at them. They're wide-awake and alert. Maybe they'll learn to nod their heads to the beat."

Jeremy laughed. "You're goofy, man. Why don't you play the piano for her and see what happens?"

Diego looked thoughtful. "Hey, I have to practice anyway. Good idea."

Some of the approved toys were again demonstrated with the puppies. Then they planned their next outing, which would be a hockey game. The club would obtain complimentary tickets for the raisers and their accompanying family members.

As Aloha lay quietly by his side, Diego found himself stroking her head and sweetly praising her. He was so enchanted with her. She responded by lifting her head off her paws and nudging him with her wet nose. Then she broke the spell and smiled up at him, wrinkling her little nose.

Chapter Nine

Everything has its wonders, even darkness and silence;
And I learn, whatever state I am in, therein to be content.
—Helen Keller

"Miss Kimberly Louise, please press my fingers if you can hear me."

From a shadowy distance, she could hear the comforting request of an unfamiliar voice. Slowly she squeezed his fingers. "Who are you?" she wondered aloud as she turned in the direction of his sound.

"Oh Mama, you're awake! Thank you, Jesus!"

She thought she recognized the voice of her daughter Julia.

Kimberly Louise looked toward Julia's voice, but she saw only dark clusters.

"Julia, are you there? Please turn on the light so I can see you. Where are we?" she asked.

The doctor took her hand in his and spoke softly. "Ma'am, I am Dr. Serrano and we are in Memorial Hospital. You have suffered an accident and had a brain concussion, sending you into a coma for several days. Do you understand what I am saying?

Oh Dear God, she thought. *This must be a terrible dream.*

"Dr. Serrano, I can hear you. But why have you bandaged my eyes? And why are my hands tied down to the bed?"

"Mama, your eyes are not bandaged. Your hands were secured for your own protection during your coma," offered her son, John Henry.

John Henry was here too? Who else was in this room?

"Where are my grandbabies?" she questioned. Her startled blue eyes searched the room. "I cannot see anyone. Please turn on the light."

The room suddenly became very quiet. Kimberly Louise's adult children exchanged nervous glances with Dr. Serrano. Julia wiped away a tear and looked away.

"Miss Kimberly Louise," he began, "you are experiencing what we hope to be a temporary loss of sight due to the trauma of your accident. At this point we do not know the extent of the injury to your optic nerves, which is causing you some visual impairment. Can you tell me what you can see?"

"What accident?" She was clearly agitated now. "I don't remember any accident."

Patiently, Dr. Serrano and her children related the car accident on Jekyll Island. They told her about her injuries and those of her good friends, Mimi and David.

Besides her damaged optic nerve fibers, Kimberly Louise had suffered neck whiplash and several broken ribs. Mimi had a fractured hip and arm. David broke his arm and had many facial bruises. The two passengers in the jeep were in critical condition.

"Lord have mercy," she moaned. "I can't remember any of it. Will my dear friends be all right?"

Dr. Serrano assured her that they would recover. Julia studied her mother with terrible sadness in her eyes. She was troubled at Kimberly Louise's apparent lack of concern for herself and her loss of sight.

Kimberly Louise had always challenged life's obstacles. She refused to surrender herself to negative fears about the unknown.

"Julia dear, perhaps if you give me my reading glasses I'll be able to see a little better." Kimberly Louise gingerly and slowly turned her head toward her daughter's voice. Julia was grateful that her mother could not see the stream of tears falling from her eyes.

When Kimberly Louise put on her glasses, she saw only a white backdrop with dark shapes. She blinked and felt the panic rising up through her chest. She covered her face with trembling hands as her mind shorted out. Reasoning with herself she struggled for control, collecting all remaining fragments of calm she could gather. After several minutes,

Kimberly Louise drew in a long cleansing breath, straightened her spine, and felt a quick jolt of pain in her neck. With a dainty sweep of her hand, she brushed a loose strand of auburn hair from her face.

"I'm quite certain this optic nerve damage will clear up by itself in a matter of days," she calmly assured her distraught family. For one brief moment, she gave them her eyes and they could see her pain and fear.

She smiled bravely at them. Inwardly, she crumbled.

Chapter Ten

Of all earthly music, that which reaches farthest into Heaven is the beating of a truly loving heart.

—Henry Ward Beecher

Diego awoke very early and tried to remember why he was so excited. Shaking the fogginess from his head, he heard his parents talking softly in the next room. Then he saw his packed suitcase on the floor and realized that they were flying to Orlando today!

Aloha lay watching him from the corner of her eye. Once she understood that they were getting up this early, she stretched luxuriously and rolled over on her back to have her tummy rubbed. Diego quickly complied, then raced her downstairs to feed her breakfast.

This was the first day of their two-week Christmas vacation and they were leaving the dismal rainy Oregon weather for a trip to sunny Florida. *That rocks*! thought Diego. Four years ago they visited Disneyland, but none of them had been to Walt Disney World or Universal Studios. Diego was thrilled to be able to spend his Christmas vacation there. The most exciting part was the fact that he would be the first one in his Puppy Raiser Club to fly with his dog!

Aloha would be riding in the cabin of the airplane with them. She had all her papers, her toys and grooming supplies and her leashes and crate. Diego put on her green and white puppy jacket with "Guide Dog Puppy in Training" written in bold letters. It was important that other passengers know she was a working dog and respect her training process.

After a hurried round of juice, coffee and muffins, they were settling in the car.

"*Mamá, ya vámanos,*" pleaded Diego. When he was nervous or excited, he often reverted to Spanish. Now he was urging his mother to get in. Five minutes later, they were on their way to the airport. Aloha sat on the floor between Diego and Clara, her tail thumping in anticipation. As always, she was on the leash as she traveled in the vehicle.

When they reached the airport, Diego closed his eyes and said a little prayer for a safe journey. He had flown twice before, once to Disneyland and recently to Guadalajara. Clara had only flown once, and was very excited about this trip.

"Do you think we'll see Mt. Hood from the plane?" she asked her older brother.

"I think so. And maybe Mt. Bachelor and Mt. Rainier too," replied Diego, remembering how he had skied those three mountains last year.

At the airport Aloha received a great deal of attention. Many people asked if they could pet her. Sometimes he allowed it when she was lying quietly by his side. But while she was working, or walking on leash, he couldn't permit the distractions.

"I'm sorry, I can't stop right now but if you see us later in the boarding area you may pet her," he apologized to an older lady calling to him as they hurried to the gate. Everyone who stopped to ask questions commented on her beauty and poise. Diego smiled when he realized just how proud of her he was.

Once they were airborne, everyone relaxed and enjoyed the flight. Aloha curled up at his feet and slept most of the way to Florida. Diego read his new book and played a card game with Clara. Maria Teresa and Ernesto read, slept and answered the children's questions. The flight was smooth and enjoyable. Diego thought the food was delicious and wondered why his friends complained about airplane meals.

Ernesto had reserved a rental car, which they picked up in the airport. Diego and Clara requested a convertible, but their father explained that Aloha probably would not have wanted so much wind blowing on her.

"Come on, Papá, we've never ridden in a convertible. Aloha would love it!" argued Diego.

"She'll also love this van where she can finally stretch out between your feet and the seat," countered Ernesto.

They drove away to the hotel in the roomy van, and Maria Teresa commented that everyone needed to get out into the balmy weather and run off the travel fatigue. They immediately noticed the tall palm trees and tropical flowers lining the freeways. Ernesto pointed out the shorter palmetto trees and showed them the Spanish moss covering the live oaks. The air felt steamy and the colors seemed softer in this part of the country.

"Mamá, can you believe we are actually here in this warm weather?" asked Diego.

"It's warm and humid," said Maria Teresa, brightening up, "just like my hometown in Mexico. This brings back wonderful memories." She recounted her childhood as a very young girl in Campeche, Mexico, where she had lived on the beach with a warm ocean, hot days, and high humidity.

"*Preciosa*, you can swim here too and show the children how to find the most beautiful seashells," said her husband. "In a few days we will travel to Cape Canaveral and you can spend the afternoon in the ocean at Cocoa Beach."

"When will we go to Disney World?" Clara was worried.

"Darling, we have two weeks and we'll have time to see it all," laughed her father.

Their hotel had several large swimming pools and beautiful gardens, which they enjoyed for the rest of the afternoon. Aloha's little nose was busy sniffing out new odors. Diego found a stretch of grass and ran her on the long-line leash. He pulled her rubber ring from the bag so he and Clara could play tug with her.

Aloha leapt into the air and caught the rubber ring. This was one of her favorite toys. She shook it fiercely back and forth. Diego grabbed it and tugged on it roughly, trying to free it from her mouth. Aloha held her ground, and Diego let her win.

Besides enhancing the dogs' teeth strength, this toy enabled the raisers to bond with their puppies.

When she began to pant, Diego called out to her. "Aloha, that's enough." She immediately stopped the game. "Good girl," he said.

He leaned over and gave her a kiss. It was such a small gesture, but nothing made her happier than his words of praise and simple acts of love. He held her very close in a huge hug.

Diego took her inside the air-conditioned room. Moments later she was dozing peacefully.

"Papá, I love Florida!" exclaimed Diego. "We're going to have a wonderful vacation here. Thank you so much for bringing us."

"Me too," added Clara. She crawled up on her father's lap, ready to cuddle at a moment's notice.

Maria Teresa and Ernesto exchanged smiles. They too knew this Christmas would be truly special for all of them. Sharing it with Aloha made it even more so.

"Hasn't he come a long way since Aloha arrived?" whispered Maria Teresa, beaming. She was thinking about Diego's poise and confidence at the airport as he answered other passenger's questions about his dog.

"Sí, querida," replied Ernesto. *"Ella es nuestro milagro.* (She is our miracle.) I can see Diego developing into a confident young man."

Aloha, knowing that she was being praised, opened her huge, intelligent eyes and wrinkled her nose in her peculiar smile. Maria Teresa laughed and rubbed her tummy. Aloha drifted back into dreamland.

Chapter Eleven

Blessed are the pure in heart,
for they will see God.

—Matthew 5:8

Diego, Clara and their parents concluded that Disney World and Epcot Center were awesome! The children were bewitched at every turn, and they loved introducing Aloha to each new experience. Of course she did not join them on the frightening roller coaster rides or speedy electrical games, but she was allowed to accompany them to the exhibits and shows. In most states, the guide puppies can go wherever a blind person might go; places where other dogs are not normally allowed. Giant theme parks like Disney World and Epcot Center are familiar with this policy, but some restaurants and malls are not. The raisers are taught to request permission to enter with their guide dogs in training, and Diego was finding this to be challenging and fun. He began to enjoy the interaction with the adults and posed his questions thoughtfully.

"Hi, Sir. We're here with our guide puppy in training. She already knows restaurant etiquette. Is it okay to bring her in with us?"

He was always received with a warm smile and an affirmative response. This newfound confidence was a wonderful accomplishment for Diego.

Aloha behaved well in restaurants, but every so often she would express an interest in people food. She was not supposed to be fed by any other means than her bowl, not even snacks or treats. This sometimes frustrated her and Diego. From her vantage point under the table, the food odors reached her from all sides, but she had reached the point where she simply twitched her nose, lifted her eyelids, yawned and took a nap.

After the Escobár family's visits to Disney World, Epcot and Cape Canaveral, they reached their ocean destination of Cocoa Beach. Quickly they settled into a quaint motel, and since it was still early, they all wanted to rent bicycles. But what would they do with Aloha? Diego remembered from his puppy raising training that there are some situations where it isn't possible to take the pup with you, and that is okay. He offered to stay behind, but his father spoke up.

"Why don't you three go biking and Aloha and I will stay back here and rest," he suggested. "I know she'd like a long nap in her crate."

They agreed, and each one spent the afternoon doing what he or she really wanted to do.

Later that afternoon they all took a walk to the beach, sat in the sand and listened to the crashing waves. The soft breeze stirred the tall beach grasses as they walked into the ocean. This was Aloha's first time exploring a warm ocean. Diego and Jeremy had taken the pups to Gold Beach in Oregon, but it was much colder than this Atlantic Ocean water. She approached the water's edge tentatively and stuck her curious nose right into the salt water. After shaking herself vigorously, she ventured in a little further. Diego and Clara encouraged her, one of them always keeping a strong hold on the long leash. Soon she was prancing around, bouncing and springing, with her front legs and face in the water, and her hind legs leaping into the air. She was enjoying herself and kept the kids chortling with glee.

Two days later they drove north to St. Augustine, Florida. This old Spanish town was founded in 1565, making it the oldest city in the United States. The streets were made of cobblestone, which the children decided made walking more fun. The town had been defended over the years by a military post, El Castillo de San Marcos, and that was still standing. As they explored St. Augustine, they felt like they were walking through Spain or Mexico. Ernesto had kept this part of the trip a secret, even from his wife.

"I brought you to St. Augustine because here we will be

able to honor one of our Mexican traditions," he exclaimed excitedly. "Tomorrow evening we'll be participating in a '*Posada*,' just like your mother and I have done when we've spent Christmas in Mexico in years past."

All three smiled with pleasure. "Oh Papá, I remember the Posada story from a book you read us. Will we sing the songs in Spanish too?" inquired Clara, her bright brown eyes aglow.

"Yes, *mi hijita* (my little daughter), but they will have the words printed out for you to follow." This pleased them because the children did not know the words to the old traditional songs.

The *Posada* was a delightful procession led by two children, carrying a small platform bearing replicas of Joseph and Mary riding a burro. They gathered at the Cathedral, and together they walked through the cobbled streets of St. Augustine, carrying lighted candles and singing the "Litany of the Virgin" as they arrived at the door of the assigned house. In this Spanish tradition the group asked for lodging for Mary and Joseph. They were refused admittance at every home until finally, one of the owners recognized his guests. After entering the last house, inside El Castillo de San Marcos, they all knelt around the manger scene, offering songs of welcome, Ave Marias and a prayer. It was a lovely ritual and the older Escobárs enjoyed participating in this tradition once again.

"This is my favorite place," murmured Maria Teresa. "I'm so happy the children can see true Spanish culture here in the United States."

Diego called Jeremy to wish him a Merry Christmas, and to share his exciting adventures. Jeremy was happy to hear from him and brought him up to date on his Christmas vacation.

"Hey Diego, you're lucky you're away. Last weekend they made us switch dogs, and 'Miss Know-it-all' got Alma. I know my puppy missed me bad."

Diego laughed. He knew Wendy would do a good job with Alma, but she had such an irritating superior attitude.

"Did you get Aztec?" asked Diego.

"Yup, and he was cool. He reminds me of Aloha. Same personality. He's really a sweet dog, and he obeyed me great."

Diego smiled on his end of the phone, as he saw how much Jeremy loved the Puppy Raising Program. He took such good care of Alma, and loved Aloha almost as much as Diego did.

Could this be the same buddy who got in big trouble last year for toilet papering the cemetery? Diego thought of how many times Jeremy had to stay after school during grade school for not finishing his work. Now he seemed more mature and responsible, and Diego knew that Alma was the reason.

"Hey Diego. Come on back. We miss you guys. Have a great Christmas. Tell Clara I have her present under the tree."

Smiling, Diego returned to the family domino game. Clara looked up. "You lost your turn and I'm beating you bad," she giggled.

The next day they ate lunch at a Cuban restaurant and dinner in an outdoor Spanish café. Ernesto and Maria Teresa spoke Spanish many times throughout the day, and at times Diego and Clara joined them.

"Muchas gracias por todo," Diego said to the server after they finished dinner. "*Me encantó la cena*. (I loved dinner.)"

Tired and satisfied, they walked home to their little inn on San Marcos Boulevard. This trip was filled with so many awesome experiences. Aloha had ridden an airplane, a trolley, a bus, and visited the Cathedral in St. Augustine. Then she joined them for the *Posada* celebration. Through it all, she had behaved beautifully. Diego took a few moments in the Cathedral to give thanks.

"*Gracias, Díos Mío, por todo lo que me has dado*. (Thank you, my Lord, for all you have given me.)"

Diego knew that he would always hold the memories of that special Christmas close to his heart.

Chapter Twelve

He who conquers others is strong;
He who conquers himself is mighty.

—Lao Tzu

"Miss Kimberly Louise, when we go blind the part of the brain that allows seeing isn't stimulated. But the part that allows us to visualize, the parietal lobe, is able to be stimulated. So by picturing things, we can retrieve memories. The eye works somewhat like a camera taking pictures, and these pictures are imprinted in your brain." Dr. Serrano was attempting to explain the sight loss process to Kimberly Louise and her daughter.

"That explains why my dreams are filled with colors and images. So because all visual images are recorded in the mind, it can play them back through dreams exactly as they were seen years ago. And I have lots of memories to draw on," she said, comprehending perfectly.

"Yes, that's correct. When you see something, your eyes

only transmit the information to the brain. The eyes don't convert the information into pictures or images, but the brain does and stores them. Then the brain can call up what you have seen, and can let you see it all over again."

Kimberly Louise listened attentively, her hands folded on her lap. Her daughter watched her with concern, wondering if her mother felt uncomfortable in Dr. Serrano's office.

"Vision normally dominates hearing, smell, touch and taste," he continued. "It's not true that when one sense is missing the rest grow stronger. You simply learn to focus more on the others and to trust them."

It had been so difficult watching her mother wrestling with her feelings of inadequacy and frustration. Julia remembered a conversation they had last week.

"Julia, if I had only known I was going to lose my sight, I could have taken the time to review all the familiar things I love," she said, her eyes filling. "I would have walked the beach and admired the ocean's foam. I could have studied the patterns in the moss dangling from the branches of the oak trees. I certainly would have tried to memorize the beauty of the rising orange sun behind me on the causeway and the river shimmering in the late afternoon sunlight. But most importantly, I would have committed to memory the faces of my loved ones."

Tears sprang to Julia's eyes as she listened to her mother. She hugged her close, understanding that Kimberly Louise did not want compassion or pity. She found it hard to distinguish the fine line between love and condolence.

"And Julia," she added quietly, her eyes deep and serious, "there is no substitute for the interchange of a smile."

The first few weeks after she returned home from the hospital, Kimberly Louise experienced an enormous sense of loss and depression. She told her family her blindness was like falling from a hilltop.

"I've gone from mountains of triumph to valleys of failure, at least in my mind's eye. Life has suddenly taken me on a long ride, and no one knows the outcome. I hate being so dependent on everyone. It's humiliating for me to have to ask you for help in everything I do."

"Mama, don't talk about failure. Your world is changing and we want to help you. Please don't turn us away," pleaded Julia. She and John Henry worried that their independent mother would combat her feelings of helplessness by giving up. She tried to withdraw from them, but they took turns staying with her and encouraging her. She became very angry at life's injustices, at people with vision, and especially at anyone trying to help her.

She felt slow and clumsy, and was humiliated when she dropped food on the floor or knocked over a glass filled with water. She never went out her front door without asking whoever accompanied her if her clothes were inside out. She considered herself frumpy and disheveled, even though she was not. Eating every meal made her feel self-conscious. She cried a lot; crying made her feel better. She knew she was deeply rooted in self-pity.

"Every morning I wake up and the first thought I have is that I'll never see my grandchildren smile again." Kimberly Louise ranted, her deep blue eyes flashing.

"But they'll always be close to you, Mama." John Henry reached out to her. "We're all here for you, and together we'll get through this."

Kimberly Louise realized she was making it very difficult for her loved ones. She tried to face her blindness with dignity. She grieved the realization of her loss of spontaneity: jumping into the car and taking off for the beach on the spur of the moment. She mourned the inability to see her beloved family's faces and read their emotions.

Their family therapist assured them this was normal and gave her children advice on how to deal with it.

"Try not to respond to the anger and self-pity," she said, "but show her that, within limits, help is possible. She will need to relearn the vast knowledge that she already has."

"My mother loves walking, swimming and most forms of exercise. Should we encourage her to get back into that once her ribs are healed?" asked Julia.

"Of course. Exercise is one of the best ways to handle anger by relieving stress and giving her the ability to focus her energies on useful activities."

As Kimberly Louise healed physically, she accepted her fate. She understood that the trauma she suffered caused her optic nerve to atrophy: the fibers of her optic nerve were dying and wasting away. She realized that the resulting visual impairment was near total blindness.

"Doctor, I'm going to be blind for the rest of my life, aren't I?" she asked, her eyes clouding slightly.

"No one knows that for sure, Miss Kimberly Louise. Miracles happen every day," he answered sincerely.

"Today I'm seeing a smoky white fog with my eyes open or closed. Yesterday I saw large, dark images. And sometimes I see brilliant flashes of greens, blues, reds and yellows. Like a kaleidoscope. Why is this happening to me?"

Dr. Serrano explained to her that all these images were replayed through the brain as it recalled stored information, and that this was a normal occurrence.

"But Dr. Serrano, I feel like I'm wearing goggles with Vaseline smeared over the plastic. It's so disconcerting," she protested.

"Miss Kimberly Louise, you cannot control the extent of your blindness. But you can control the state of your mind. We will work together and your mind will accept your limitations with time," he consoled her gently.

"And I always have my dreams," she smiled sweetly. "I still see everything and everyone in Technicolor in my dreams."

He spoke to her about a rehabilitation center that

included mobility and orientation training. It was located in Warm Springs, Georgia. She would learn how to get around with various travel aids. They would also offer her Braille reading, typing, handwriting, grooming, cooking and cleaning, recreation and counseling.

"You will learn to walk back into the world unafraid," he promised her.

Very slowly Kimberly Louise realized that she had to fight this setback. She knew that her hopes and dreams were worth pursuing even when the chances of success were not always guaranteed. She had always been determined to challenge limits, learn, grow and live her life to the fullest. She possessed an inner strength that had enabled her to fight until she triumphed over the odds. Her blindness was her greatest hurdle and would require extraordinary courage.

She called her family together. After thanking them for their love and encouragement during the past months, she made her announcement.

"I've enrolled in the Roosevelt Warm Springs Institute for Rehabilitation, and they said I can start in three weeks. When I return, I should be walking with a cane and hopefully, heading toward independence. In the meantime, I want you to know that I'm slowly crossing the bridge from self-pity to hope. You have all helped me greatly, bless your hearts. Now I'm going away to regain my independence."

Her voice reflected pure smiling confidence.

Chapter Thirteen

Do not spoil what you have by desiring what you have not; but remember that what you now have was once among the things only hoped for.

—Epicurus

Aloha was ready for her second test at the campus. Their group leader Nancy was waiting for them when they arrived early Saturday morning. Some of the other raisers had already finished testing their dogs; others were waiting to go into the room. Soon it would be Aloha's turn. Diego was nervous.

"Jeremy, tell me again what Alma did wrong," he pleaded with his friend.

"She started to eat some food off the table and the puppy advisor walked over and corrected her. Then she barked at the trash can," he groaned.

The puppies were placed in a room with a one way glass so they could be observed but not see out. Many temptations were placed within their reach: items they had already been trained to ignore, such as snacks on a table, furniture to jump on, garbage in a bin, and socks and shoes to chew. Each puppy was left alone to explore the room and his or her behavior was monitored. Alma and others had tried to chew, eat, or jump up on the furniture, thinking they were alone and unobserved. The puppy advisor was a trainer who would suddenly appear in the room to show the puppy that unacceptable behavior would not be tolerated. By hitting the wall loudly and startling the dogs, she got them to stop the activity immediately. When the dogs settled down again, their raisers were allowed to go into the room and praise them.

The first time Aloha had been tested several months back she nibbled on the snacks and jumped on the chair. Diego felt sure that by now she had been corrected on those behaviors. He wondered how she would do with the garbage. Her curiosity often got the better of her, and he knew she would want to smell it.

"Diego, your turn. Good luck," said Nancy.

Diego and his family were watching through the glass. Aloha slowly walked around the room and took it all in. Diego wondered if she remembered being there before. He found himself holding his breath as the seconds ticked away. Aloha walked to the table and sniffed the snacks, but did not touch them. She eyed the chair and sofa, but kept all four feet on the floor.

"Yes!" whispered Diego, louder than he thought. "Keep it

up, *muchachita*. You're my good girl." Standing next to him, he saw Clara smile and cross her fingers for good luck.

Aloha walked over to the garbage bin. Using her extremely sensitive nose to smell it from a distance, she then stuck it inside the bin for a closer sniff.

"Aaaarraaahhhhhhh!" The trainer rushed through the door, grabbed her collar, and pulled her back.

Aloha backed up, quite startled, and immediately lay down. She began to yawn widely, looking all around the room. The trainer told Diego that he could now go in and praise her.

"That's right, Aloha," he cooed to her as he hugged her and scratched behind her ears. She wiggled her back and tail with pleasure and relief at seeing Diego. "You are doing so well. That's my good girl." Then he left the room.

Outside the glass, Nancy explained that dogs often yawn when they are nervous or worried. After Diego left, Aloha stayed in her prone position, yawning from time to time. Eventually, she got up and walked slowly around the room, sniffing cautiously and listening.

Finally, Diego was allowed to go and get her. She had done well. In fact, all the dogs in their Puppy Raiser Club proved to be good students. They had learned their commands, exhibited self-control, ignored the distractions for the most part and trusted their instincts.

Then Diego remembered last weekend's camping trip.

He, Jeremy and several other friends had taken their dogs for an overnight camping trip near Silver Falls in the Cascade Mountains. After darkness fell, they sat by the campfire and enjoyed the beautiful night. Stars were everywhere, tiny white dots in the brilliant sky.

A couple, friends of some parents in the group, approached their campsite. Alma sat up in a flash and began a low, rumbling growl deep in her throat.

"Alma, enough!" scolded Jeremy. "Stop that now!"

Alma obeyed and lay down at his side. Jeremy turned to Diego.

"That's the second time she's done that out here. Do you think she's spooked?"

"I don't know. Let's watch her closely."

After they were snuggled into their sleeping bags and almost asleep, Alma heard a rustle in the bushes. She barked sharply and moved to the door of the tent, as if to protect the boys. Jeremy pulled her back to his side and spoke quietly to her in the darkness.

"She never does this at home. I'm worried. Maybe we need to tell Nancy."

Nancy worked with Jeremy to correct this behavior. But now Diego realized that Alma had alarm barked, or barked a warning, again today at the trash can. He wondered if Jeremy had noticed.

After the testing was over, many of the raisers stayed on

campus to watch a graduation ceremony. This was the day that a class of sight-impaired graduates would complete training with their own guide dogs. The raisers walk them on stage and present them to the graduates. The raisers have not seen their puppies for several months, since the day they left them there to train at the facility. The graduates have spent about four weeks living with the dogs in their rooms on campus, and now are ready to take them home.

Diego and his family sat with the other members of their Puppy Raiser Club. The ceremony was beautifully done, genuinely moving and emotional. Diego felt a huge lump in his throat watching other raisers present their precious dogs to the new owners. Many tears were shed in the audience, even by those who did not know the people or raise the dogs. Diego's mother reached for his hand and gave it a soft squeeze.

"*Yo entiendo, mi hijito* (I understand, my son)," she spoke lovingly. "When it is your turn, you too will be brave and proud."

Diego fought back a deep wave of sadness. He knew he was doing this for an excellent cause, but he rebelled at the thought of giving Aloha up. Watching the graduates' faces light up as they received and embraced their dogs was worth so much, yet Diego knew his pain of losing her would be too deep. This ceremony brought back the words his mother had spoken to him a few days before Aloha arrived at their home last year.

"My son, remember that this puppy will be on loan to us from God. We've been chosen to raise her, give her the foundations that she'll need and teach her how to get along in the world. Raising her is a gift of service to others. It will be your privilege to love her and care for her, but she is not ours to keep."

He thought about how the sweet and sad in life were often interwoven. Diego was beginning to understand how impossible it was to see around corners and up hills; how every day was made up of the unknown. At that moment, he knew how much it could hurt to love something when you knew you would lose it.

He returned his thoughts to the ceremony.

"I'm not ready to let Aloha go yet. Will I ever be able to give her up?" he asked his mother.

"Yes, because you are noble and loving," she replied.

He only hoped that he would be able to visit Aloha from time to time. Better not think about that now. Just then Aloha raised her head off her paws and studied his face. She thumped her tail on his foot.

What doesn't she know about me? he thought with a sad smile. "Yes, baby girl, I love you too," he whispered tenderly.

Chapter Fourteen

Each one should use whatever gift he has received to serve others, faithfully administering God's grace in its various forms.

—1Peter 4:10

Diego slowly opened his eyes. It was dark, but he could feel Aloha's eyes staring into his face. He thought it was too early to take her outside to relieve herself, so he closed his eyes and pretended to go back to sleep. She waited patiently a few moments, then moved closer and licked his hand hanging off the bed. Diego tried to breathe like someone asleep but chuckled inwardly, knowing she would not be fooled. Sure enough, in another moment she was licking his face.

"Aloha, it's not even six o'clock yet," he grumbled. "Do you have to do your business this early, or are you hungry? It's too early to feed you."

He switched on the light and discovered it was 5:30 a.m. She whined slightly so Diego took her downstairs and into the back yard. She did her business and then walked quickly to her food dish.

"I don't know if I should feed you so early, but this time I will. I think I'll check with Nancy and ask her whether you're pulling a fast one on me," giggled Diego as he gave her ears a gentle tug. Aloha turned her liquid brown eyes on him and gave him a wrinkled nose smile.

She was almost a year old now. She no longer looked like a puppy, except for her inquisitive face, but she wasn't the size of a grown dog either. Aloha knew all her commands and obeyed very well. She was nearing the end of the Raiser Program training period. All the puppies in her group, including her littermates, could be recalled to the campus at any time to begin the final training with the instructors.

"Jeremy, have you heard anything yet about sending Alma back to the campus?" asked Diego one afternoon after baseball practice.

"Nope, and I'm crossing my fingers that she'll be the last to go."

"So am I. Hey, we got them the same day, so maybe we can return them the same day."

The boys figured they still had several months before that day arrived, and summer was almost here. Jeremy and Alma were going to fly to New York to visit relatives. Diego and

Clara would be going to camp in July, and to their great delight, the camp staff had given them permission to bring Aloha. The boys were also busy preparing their end of the year school projects.

Diego had a paper due about his most unusual adventure with a best friend. He had decided to write about his friendship with Aloha and the companionship that she offered him. He would entitle his essay "Giving Back to the Community" because that was what he was doing with her.

Diego wrote about the first day he saw her, and how excited he felt as he embraced her. He described Aloha's amusing games with her big toy bone.

"Even as a puppy she carried this big toy bone in her mouth," he wrote. "It was wider than she was, but she could hold it between her teeth and still run up and down the stairs. She held on tight when we tried to pry it from her. It was her favorite game."

He wrote about problems they faced during the training period.

"My sister Clara uses 'scrunchies' to hold her hair in a ponytail. Aloha found them wherever she dropped them, and she ate them! A while later we would hear an awful gagging sound and see Aloha's body jerking. Then she would throw up her last meal and the scrunchy. Once she threw up a washcloth, too. Several times we found cotton balls in her vomit. After a while, we just kept towels close by so we could cover the floor when we heard her start to gag."

Diego ended his essay with fond remarks about their fellowship.

"I think Aloha has taught me courage. If she could leave her family and come to us without a whimper, I could work on my small fears. Now I feel comfortable raising my hand and answering questions in school. I know it's okay to study and learn as much as I can."

"Also, Aloha was so comfortable with strangers and she helped me feel good about talking with them and explaining her training process. I watch her confidently obey her commands, and show us what a great leader dog she's becoming. Then I know I can be a leader in my own small world, and that feels good."

The final paragraph of his essay dealt with their friendship.

"Aloha has shown me unconditional love. I've never had a friend like her, one who loves me just for being in her life. She wants to please, and she wants to be with me. She is giving up many doggy traits so she will be able to focus on her blind partner. She loves and trusts me in everything we do, and I love and trust her. Soon I will have taken her as far as I can, and she'll have to move on to learn more and become the dog she was bred to be. Giving her up to the school will be the hardest day of my life."

Diego put down his pen and reached under his chair.

"Aloha, my baby girl, I appreciate you so much. I think you've made me a better person."

Rolling over to face him, her eyes drooped half closed and she stretched on her back, waiting for her tummy to be scratched.

"Isn't it great that dogs don't have to worry about the future?" he asked her. "You just enjoy each fun day as it comes, don't you *muchachita*. Teach me to be like you."

Aloha grunted and waved her front paws in the air, telling him that she wasn't quite ready to have the tummy rub end. Diego laughed as he hugged her close.

"We're so lucky to have her in our lives," he turned to tell Clara as she walked into the room.

"Diego, do you think she will remember us after she goes back to the campus?" Clara's brown eyes suddenly brimmed over with tears. She wiped them away with the back of her hand as they began to run down her cheeks.

"I think she'll always remember us, just like we'll never forget her," he answered. He gradually turned his head away so she wouldn't see his tear. "And I know she'll always love us too," he added, very quietly.

Chapter Fifteen

When you get into a tight place and everything goes against you, never give up, for that is just the place and time that the tide will turn.

—Harriet Beecher Stowe

The day was hot and humid. The boys had convinced Diego's parents to drive them to the waterpark near Cannon Beach and leave them there for the day. Jeremy's parents would pick them up in the afternoon. As they passed the ocean on their way home, the Escobárs decided to take Aloha to the beach for a refreshing swim.

Aloha loved the water and eagerly raced into the waves, pulling Ernesto close behind her. His wife laughed with delight and made a video of their antics.

"I'm sure Diego will be happy we had the camera in the car," she giggled. "Let's surprise him with this video after he has taken Aloha back to Guide Dogs," she added wistfully.

They enjoyed their picnic lunch while Aloha napped under the umbrella.

As they climbed from the car into their driveway, covered with sand, dirt and sweat, Ernesto suggested giving Aloha a bath. Ten minutes later he was hosing her off in the back yard with warm water as his wife gently held her by the skin on her neck. Aloha enjoyed this and shook the water off her back, spraying them both.

The sound of the phone disrupted their project. Ernesto put down the hose and went it to answer it, while Maria Teresa squeezed the water from Aloha's back and legs. She picked up a towel and began to wipe her down.

"You smell so clean, Aloha," she cooed to the dog. "Once you dry off in the sun I'll feed you dinner."

Aloha's ears perked up at the word "dinner." Wagging her tail with anticipation, she stood obediently during the drying ritual.

Ernesto was still speaking on the phone in a low tone of voice and furrowing his brow. Maria Teresa wondered if Jeremy and Diego were calling with bad news.

At that moment screams shrieked across the neighbors' yard. She recognized the sounds coming from Ginny, her neighbors' little daughter.

"Ginny, what happened?" she called to her.

When Ginny did not respond, she hurried to the fence and saw her doubled over, holding her upper arm and crying hysterically. To her surprise, the three-year-old was alone in the yard.

Maria Teresa rushed through the gate that separated their yards and scooped her into her arms. She examined the child's arm and discovered what she thought was a wasp sting. Trying to comfort the frightened little girl, she looked up to see Ginny's mother dashing through the kitchen door.

"Dear Lord, what happened?" she asked breathlessly. "I was upstairs in my room for just a moment and heard her shrieking."

"I think it's a wasp sting, Shirley."

They finally calmed Ginny and took her inside to care for her arm. Suddenly Maria Teresa remembered Aloha.

"Gotta run. I left Aloha alone in my yard," she explained.

She dashed back through the gate and found her husband looking around bewildered.

"Where's Aloha?" He was confused.

"Oh no," moaned his wife. "She was just here drying off, but Ginny screamed and I rushed over to help her."

They ran through the front yard into the street. There was no sign of Aloha.

"Wait, you left the fence gate open when you went next door. Maybe she went over there," he suggested hopefully.

They retraced their steps and realized with dismay that the neighbors' gate to the street was ajar. Aloha probably followed her over and then walked out through the gate.

With heavy hearts, they went out to look for her. They took different routes, calling her name again and again. After searching for about an hour, each one returned home. Ernesto found Maria Teresa sitting on the porch steps, her head in her hands. She began to sob as he gathered her in his arms.

"It's all my fault," she cried. "I didn't close the fence gate after me. How could I have been so stupid?"

"We were tired and dirty and wanted to clean her up for Diego. We'll find her, *querida*. Someone will pick her up and call the pound."

"*Diós Mío*! She doesn't have her collar on. Nobody will know where she belongs," she groaned. "And I will be in big trouble because I took off her collar. We were never supposed to do that. I wasn't thinking."

"Maybe they'll look at her ears and find her tattoos. Don't give up hope," he offered.

"What if she gets hit by a car. *Ay yi yi*, we're in such trouble!"

"We have to call Nancy right away. Remember, she said if anything ever happens to the dogs, we have to let her know."

They phoned Nancy, their Puppy Raiser Club leader. She calmly told them to call the pounds and animal shelters in the area. She would notify the other members of the club, as well as Guide Dogs for the Blind. They agreed to check back with her in an hour.

The Escobárs divided up the phone calls. Fortunately they reached Jeremy's parents before they left to pick up the boys. They agreed not to tell Diego and Jeremy anything until they returned home.

When the boys arrived with Jeremy's parents, Ernesto and Maria Teresa asked them to sit down in the living room and they explained everything.

Diego listened to the story with disbelief. Holding back his tears as well as he could, he closed his eyes and prayed.

"Dear God, I know You know where she is. Bring her back to me. I can't lose her now. Help us find her soon. You know how hard this is for me. I'll die if anything happens to her. Please, God. Amen."

"I'm sure she will be found safe and sound." His father spoke up in an attempt to comfort them all.

Several hours later, Diego phoned Jeremy to tell him there was no news.

"I'm really mad at my parents. How could they have done this to me?" he asked angrily.

"Hey buddy, they didn't mean to do it. Besides, she'll show up at the pound or the police station. You'll see," offered Jeremy, confused himself at the unhappy outcome of the day.

"And if we don't find her by tomorrow, we'll call the radio and television stations," he added. "You'll get her back, Diego. I know you will."

As he climbed into bed, he tried hard to believe it himself.

Chapter Sixteen

You must do the thing you think you cannot do.

—Eleanor Roosevelt

It seemed strange that she had been here only three weeks and already Kimberly Louise felt her confidence returning. As she lay resting on her bed with closed eyes and elevated legs, she thought about the school director's words to them at the first group meeting.

"Our residential school will help you open the door to society. This is accomplished through the giving and taking that can only be achieved through interaction with others who are physically impaired." He addressed the students collectively and then spoke to the various disabilities. When he addressed the visually impaired, he encouraged them with these words.

"In our school you will discover a new independence by exercising your visual memory and developing greater listening skills."

She thought about those words and smiled broadly. It was

true that she had forged a strong bond with the others with sight-impairment as they learned to perform the most elementary tasks. These new friendships gave her comfort and camaraderie. Several of the students were from the south and she knew she would have the opportunity to visit with them again.

Kimberly Louise worked with other sight-impaired students on their orientation and mobility skills. The purpose of the orientation and mobility training was to promote safe, efficient, graceful and independent movement through any environment. This included indoor and outdoor, familiar and unfamiliar. The goal was to permit the students to travel when and wherever they wished (within their capabilities) without having to rely on others.

The first two weeks were designed to promote confidence by mastering daily living skills. Kimberly Louise had always been very careful with her grooming, and was anxious to relearn how to "put on her face." She was shown how to add color to her fluorescent-light pallor by applying a powdered bronze tone to her cheeks and forehead.

"It cheers me up to try to look as nice as I can," she explained to her instructor. Janet agreed. She then showed her how to pin on her cascading curls. As she attached the plump circle of curls to her upswept auburn hair, she felt delighted with her new accomplishments.

Kimberly Louise and her classmates learned how to pour

liquids by placing a finger in the glass while pouring with the other hand. The tip of the finger showed them when the glass was almost full. To peel potatoes, they formed a bridge with their thumb and forefinger and cut inside that bridge, which kept the blade away from the hand. They were learning to cook and sew by feeling the utensils and honing their tactile skills. Less enthusiastically, they discovered that they were able to wash the laundry and vacuum by using the same method. The students wrote checks with a plastic template whose cutouts guided their pen. If they took medicine, they identified the bottles with two, three or more rubber bands.

Through hit and miss tactics, they were learning to accept their mistakes with humor. They often joked about the ugly things they didn't have to see.

"I think it's liberating not seeing an unkempt beard or a blemished face," joked Ruthie at dinner one evening.

"Or, what about a stained shirt or dirty feet," giggled Kimberly Louise.

"Seriously, though, there is something redeeming about removing the props of prejudice. We can't judge people by the way they look. Wouldn't it be nice if sighted people would relate to others disregarding how they look, their disabilities or their skin color?" said Ruthie to the others at the table.

"Yes, it would. I've been thinking a lot about that," added Marshall. "And I feel there are far more tragic circumstances than blindness. We can still love, and with all the sight in the world, the absence of love would form a handicap too terrible to imagine."

During their mobility classes, the students discovered why the white cane broadened their horizons. Used as an extension of the arm, it probed the environment by the inch or the foot, just as the eye probes it by the mile. The students learned to move the cane in an arc, going to the left as the right foot steps forward and to the right as the left foot moves. In that way, the path is explored before the foot actually steps. Each student also had an opportunity to work with the laser cane. This device senses objects more than five feet away and notifies the person through a series of vibrations.

June, a sweet woman from Tennessee who was six months pregnant, needed to complete her mobility training before her baby was born. While they were learning to use the white cane, she realized that a baby stroller would stick out further than her cane and could put the baby in danger. The staff taught her to pull the stroller behind her with the handle reversed. This kept her precious cargo safely behind her. Although this frustrated June, she agreed it was the best way to walk her baby.

The students were given classes in the Braille method of reading by touch. This system of raised dots enabled the students to read with their fingers. All the letters, numbers and punctuation of a language are reproduced as raised dots on paper, and read as the fingertips pass lightly over them. The Braille System was developed in 1824 by a French teacher and musician named Louis Braille.

Many of the students felt that Braille was too difficult to learn, and chose talking books and talking computers as their preferred reading method. The computers with talking software utilize a scanner that photographs the typewritten material and then reads it out loud. One keystroke makes the computer read the whole sentence, another the paragraph, and another, the entire document. If the typist spells a word wrong, the computer spells it out loud so that it can be corrected.

"This is much faster than Braille," said Marshall to Kimberly Louise. "It will be fun using it when we e-mail each other."

They were shown other aids such as Braille watches and telephones, talking alarm clocks and scales, key rings that beep when hands are clapped, and the Braille clothing tag. This tag, the size of a fingernail, is pinned on the labels of clothing to tell the person the color. Any student interested in learning the Braille writer or slate and stylus was given the opportunity to do so.

Kimberly Louise was thrilled with the quality of classroom instruction. She enrolled in painting and sculpturing classes, and was told she had talent. When she became frustrated, her teacher took her aside.

"Miss Kimberly Louise, did you know that the painter Degas fought deteriorating vision beginning at age thirty-six? And Monet lost his ability to distinguish colors clearly because of cataracts, which he didn't have removed until he was eighty-three."

"No, Janet, I didn't know. Thank you for reminding me that we don't only see with our eyes, but also with our imagination," said Kimberly Louise.

As she painted St. Simons beach, she retrieved from her memory the dainty shells of sea creatures, the rubbery seaweed, and the different objects washed up by the ocean. Knowing that the beach is never the same from hour to hour helped her paint it as much more than a sweep of sand, and not to worry about perfection.

"Janet, please help me with my color choices. My world is still filled with the same marvelous colors as before, but now I'm viewing them from a different perspective. Have I chosen the right colors for my beach?" asked Kimberly Louise.

"Oh, yes Ma'am. This is magnificent!" exclaimed Janet, in a voice tinged with a smile. Suddenly Kimberly Louise understood how expressive a voice can be. She didn't have to see the face to know the feelings.

"Janet, I can see your emotion running through your voice! I feel your smile and your delight!" Suddenly overcome with emotion, she let the tears fall unchecked.

"Yes, Miss Kimberly dear. You do see, and now it is

through your ears and your heart, instead of your eyes," agreed Janet, taking her student's hands in her own.

"I am using all my senses except for sight, and the image is becoming mine once again." Kimberly Louise reached over to hug her instructor. "Dear Lord, I'm beginning to heal. Thank you, Janet," she added gratefully.

And now Kimberly Louise understood that the two parts of her life, her past and her present, the carefree and the complex, had united. She was, at last, conscious of how rich and good life could be.

Chapter Seventeen

Our greatest glory is not in ever falling,
but in rising every time we fall.

—Confucius

Diego awoke very early the morning after Aloha's disappearance. He left the house to look for her, thinking she may have been trying to find her way home. He had no luck, and returned home disheartened.

During the rest of the morning he received phone calls from Nancy, the Guide Dogs for the Blind school, and several of the animal centers they had phoned the day before. His mother stayed home from the courthouse to help Diego field the calls and give him support. Around noon, he fell into a troubled sleep.

The phone rang and his mother answered on the first ring.

"Are you missing a yellow lab about a year old?" a strange voice asked her.

"Yes, we are," she said shakily. "Do you have Aloha?"

"We have a dog with no collar who has tattoos in her ears, and we got a call yesterday that a dog like her is missing. Could this be your dog?" answered the young man at the animal shelter.

"Please hold on to her. We will be right over!"

She ran to Diego's bed and shook him awake.

"*Vámanos*, Diego. I think we've found Aloha!" she cried happily.

Diego rubbed his eyes and ran to phone Jeremy, who was waiting to hear any news. They drove by his house and picked him up. Both boys were chattering excitedly as they drove to the animal shelter.

The moment they entered the parking lot of the shelter, the boys opened the doors and raced from the car, leaving Maria Teresa alone to park it. Rushing inside, they identified themselves and heard Aloha whining quietly in the background. She had been trained not to bark or yelp, and she did neither. But Diego heard fear and sadness in her voice and rushed to her side.

"Oh Aloha baby, we've found you," his words tumbled out in short phrases. "Are you okay? Let me see you."

Diego studied his sweet dog sitting quietly in the cage. As he reached down to embrace her, he heard the yelping and howling of the other dogs in their enclosed areas. Tears welled up in his eyes as he imagined his precious Aloha spending the night amidst such ruckus. He held her tightly, and felt a shiver run through her body. Jeremy was at his side, with his arm around his shoulder.

"It's all good, Dude," whispered Jeremy with a strained voice. "I'll call Guide Dogs while you tell Aloha how much we've missed her."

The ordeal was not over yet. They all went together to give Nancy the news. Ernesto and Maria Teresa took full responsibility for the accident.

"Nancy, we failed to follow procedure by taking Aloha's collar off when we bathed her. It would be terrible if Diego had to lose his dog because of our lack of judgment," began Ernesto.

"Yes, it would and I'm sure the school will take that into consideration. If you'd like, I'll drive out to Boring with you tomorrow."

"Yes!" shouted both boys simultaneously.

"We will need to take Aloha along as well. I'm sure they'll want to check her out, and they may decide to keep her for awhile," she added.

The boys exchanged distressed glances.

"Why, Nancy?" worried Diego. "You have to help us convince them that it was a mistake and we're sorry. It won't ever happen again."

Diego and his family slept badly that night. They were so afraid that he could lose Aloha. Acts of irresponsibility were not taken lightly. Diego told himself over and over that he would not have removed the collar to bathe Aloha, yet he could not stay mad at his parents. They made a big mistake, but it was just a mistake.

Their Puppy Raising Advisor was waiting for them when they arrived the following morning. A trainer hurried over to lead Aloha away to be examined by the vet. Diego's heart sank as he watched her walk away.

The advisor listened to their troubled story and realized that this blunder could be turned into a lesson for future puppy raisers. After hearing their apologies, she turned to Diego.

"Diego, I know that you have been through a lot these past forty-eight hours. A rule was broken and all of you have suffered the consequences. Your dog has been kenneled with street dogs and exposed to diseases for over a day. She must be pretty shaken up by all the disturbances and confusion she experienced there. As you know, she is a sheltered puppy who wasn't even allowed to bark."

Diego sat very still, holding his breath, afraid to blink. Jeremy watched him through the corner of his eye, aching for his friend.

"I have discovered that I learn more in life through my mistakes than through my successes. This has been a tough lesson for you and your family. I've made the decision that Aloha will continue to stay with you. But first we'll have to keep her here for a few days and evaluate her." She smiled warmly at them.

Maria Teresa wiped away her tears. "I thank you so much, Miss. How would I be able to face my son knowing he lost his dog because of me?" She buried her face in her husband's shoulder.

The advisor stood and held out her hand to the boys.

"I can see that Aloha lives with a loving family who is raising her well. We'll call you when she is ready to go home. I hope you'll enjoy the rest of the summer. School will be here all too soon."

Aloha stayed at Guide Dogs for the Blind five days. The instructors decided that she was recovering well and was still trainable. They released her on a Friday to a very grateful Diego.

The summer ended on a good note.

Chapter Eighteen

I will be with him in trouble,
I will deliver him and honor him.

—Psalm 91:15

Diego and Jeremy were sitting in the new principal's office at Highland Park Middle School. He was listening to their request to bring the puppies to school with them.

"We know our dogs won't be in the way or cause any trouble here, Mr. Johnson. They're really well-trained," began Diego.

"I'm concerned about the lunchroom activities. Will they be begging or trying to eat things off the floor or the ground?" inquired Mr. Johnson.

"Oh, no!" protested Jeremy. "They have been trained not to eat people food, and never to beg!'

Mr. Johnson smiled at the boys. They were so earnest and eager to be allowed to bring the dogs to school. Although they had brought them to classes last year, he was the new principal, and the decision would be his. He didn't want to be hasty and regret it later.

"What if they have to relieve themselves during your classes? Will you need to disrupt class to take them outside?" he asked.

Diego answered quickly. "They have already been trained to go at certain times, and can last up to six hours without their break if they have to. We'd be able to relieve them during our breaks so that won't be a problem. Last year they were much younger and they never disrupted our classes."

Mr. Johnson listened carefully to their answers. The boys seemed to have all the bases covered, and he saw no reason not to allow them to bring the dogs to school three days a week.

"Oh, thank you so much, Mr. Johnson," exclaimed Jeremy. "You will have fun with them too, and learn to love them."

The boys left the office grinning widely. They knew Mr. Johnson would be proud of how well the young dogs behaved.

As the days wore on, the boys were allowed to take their dogs to school up to four days a week. They slept at their feet during classes, accompanied them through the lunch line, and joined the other students during breaks. Just like last year, the students and faculty loved having them there. The younger students in the school enjoyed learning about the dogs' training.

"Why can't we throw the ball and let Aloha bring it to us?" demanded one classmate.

"Because balls are not on the list of approved toys," replied Diego.

"That really bites! They must miss out not having a normal life," countered his friend.

"Yeah, in some ways, but Aloha goes everywhere with the people she loves, even places that pet dogs are not allowed. She plays with other toys so she doesn't miss balls and Frisbees. She never gets left in the back yard while her owners leave for the day," said Diego.

He and Jeremy got a lot of those questions from people.

"May I give them dog biscuits?" asked a teacher.

"No, I'm sorry. Hand feeding treats to the dogs teaches them to be interested in people food. They're being trained for sight-impaired people and can't have distractions when they're leading them. They have learned to eat only out of their bowls," Jeremy pointed out.

Late fall brought shorter days and warm rains to Beaverton, Oregon. The boys were still riding their skateboards, playing soccer and doing other outdoor activities. Soon the long, rainy winter would be upon them.

Clara was very helpful with Aloha when Diego was unavailable, and she often brought her friends to the house to show them how well Aloha obeyed. Her principal at Edison Elementary School invited Diego to speak and introduce Aloha to the student body. Diego asked Clara if she would like to walk Aloha through the commands.

"Oh my gosh, Diego! Do you really mean it?" she gushed.

"Yeah, sure. You can do it," he smiled. Diego felt proud of his little sister and knew that soon she would be ready to raise her own puppy. She walked Aloha through all the commands and answered her classmates' questions with poise and knowledge.

One Saturday afternoon a group of his friends went to the Willamette River for a picnic. Jeremy and Diego took their dogs. They walked to the river and admired the wildflowers growing along the sides of the road. They stopped to pick the fat blackberries oozing in the bright sunlight. Aloha reached over to bite one off the vine.

"Aloha, enough. No!" reminded Diego. She immediately dropped it, and Diego patted her head and back. "Good girl."

Soon Alma and Aloha were splashing in the cold running water, dipping their noses in, splattering and dunking into the cold river. They were having a joyous time. Diego and Jeremy later relaxed on the grass with their tired but happy Labs.

"Hey, our dogs are more than a year now. Time is going by so fast," lamented Diego.

"I hate to think about the day we take them back to the campus. Do you ever hope that they won't pass? I do, cuz then we'd have first choice to keep them, and that would totally rock."

"Sometimes I think about what if Aloha got dropped. Remember when they told us that half the dogs don't make it? Then they are 'career changed' and we can take them back. Part of me wants her to be dropped, but the other part wants her to be a great guide dog for someone who really needs her." Diego was pensive.

"Dude, you're such a goody two shoes, always talking about doing good stuff for the rest of the world," snapped Jeremy. "We really need and love our dogs. I can't even think about anyone else right now!"

Diego was stunned by Jeremy's insult and felt his cheeks burning. As he turned to vent his resentment on Jeremy, he saw the sadness on his friend's face. He was visibly hurting just thinking about losing Alma.

He turned back to hug Aloha, and she licked his face with wet doggy kisses.

Jeremy got up and punched him lightly in the shoulder.

"Hey, we're being idiots worrying about this. We both know our dogs won't be dropped. They're too smart and totally awesome," said Jeremy.

"Hmmm, remember they told us some dogs get medical problems or get too attached to the trainer and then growl or bark at anyone coming near. Who knows, maybe our dogs are already too attached to us," countered Diego wistfully.

In spite of the warm winds and late fall sunshine, Diego's mood was somber as he rode home with the others. What would he do if Aloha were career changed? Probably rejoice and shout for joy. Then he remembered how he was constantly motivated during these months of training, knowing that Aloha would be someone's wings to freedom.

"My job is to get Aloha ready for her life as a guide. The rest is not my decision to make," he mumbled to himself.

That reasoning made him feel better as he re-focused on the group's conversation. Jeremy must have been thinking the same thing, because he nudged his shoulder, smiled and gave him a high five.

Chapter Nineteen

God whispers in our pleasures, speaks in our conscience and shouts in our pain.

—C.S. Lewis

The call came Friday afternoon. Diego answered the phone.

"Hi Diego. This is Nancy. How are you today?"

Diego's heart sank. He knew what the call was about. He didn't want to hear it.

"Fine, thanks," he managed to get out.

"Guide Dogs thinks Aloha is ready to be returned to campus. You've done an amazing job with her, and now it's their turn to work with her. Can you take her out there next Saturday afternoon?" Nancy asked gently.

"I think so. Will Jeremy take Alma too?" he replied.

"Yes, Diego. I've just spoken to him. Perhaps you can bring them together."

He felt dizzy and went to sit on his bed. He thought it felt like a movie, not his life. He picked up the leash and called to his dog.

Diego was walking Aloha through the thick pine trees in the woods she loved, but he felt no peace. His parents had suggested that he take her there for a long walk, hoping that the quiet beauty of the forest would raise his spirits. It wasn't working. Finally, he crouched down and gave her a kiss.

"*Amigüita*, will you always remember me?" he asked her, his voice raw with pain. "Next week you'll leave me and become a star and make me so proud. But I'm having a real hard time letting you go."

Suddenly Diego felt overwhelmed with sadness. He knelt over her back and circled her chest with his arms, letting the tears run down his face onto her soft fur until he could cry no more. Aloha turned her head around to watch him, licking his tears and offering her paw as if to coax him into a new game.

Diego understood now what a broken heart felt like. In the woods, surrounded by his raw grief, another realization slowly came to him. Love was the basis of all their training! Her love for him was the reason she sacrificed her instincts and obeyed him. He now understood that Aloha loved him too!

After a while, Diego stood up and took the leash.

"Aloha, let's go home." He gently kissed her nose. They set off at a fast pace, running the last few blocks. Aloha was happy with the exercise. Diego felt tired and drained.

Clara met them at the door. "Diego, Mamá wants us to wash up for supper. We're going to the baseball game and we have to hurry," she explained softly as she noticed his swollen eyes.

He gave her a weak smile and she took Aloha's leash from his hand. "I'll feed her," she offered. Diego accepted gratefully, knowing that tonight would be the last baseball game Aloha would share with them. *Unless*, he thought...*unless she gets dropped from the program and I get her back!*

He wondered why he kept considering that option. Aloha would be an excellent guide dog and he knew she would move quickly through the training stages. But try as hard as he could, the idea that she might not graduate played again and again through his mind like a song.

The family was quiet and solemn during supper. Each one of them accepted the air of sadness that clouded their spirits. Finally, Ernesto suggested that it was time to leave for the game.

Aloha accompanied them, sitting happily at Diego's feet. Soon after they arrived at the stadium, Diego found Jeremy and Alma and sat with them. Somehow, that made it easier to face the reality of the next few days. Both boys were reserved and sat with their heads in their hands, barely concentrating on the game. After the game, the two families made plans for the ride to Boring the following Saturday. Jeremy's father would take both boys and their dogs. Clara watched them through serious eyes. She couldn't keep the tears from falling. The other family members decided they would stay home. Diego didn't blame them, and secretly wished he could be spared that final "goodbye" in front of the trainers.

School was now in session and the boys took their dogs with them the following week. Their schoolmates gathered around them to wish the dogs well. Some of them put their arms around their friends' shoulders and offered them consolation and kind wishes.

On Saturday morning, Jeremy's father arrived to pick them up with both dogs' gear. They drove to the Guide Dogs for the Blind campus as the wind blew and a shower of autumn leaves fell from the trees. Both boys spent their time in the car talking quietly to Alma and Aloha.

There were other raisers saying goodbye to their dogs. Diego discovered that the adults were not embarrassed to show their emotions. They wept openly and hugged their dogs close to them. The trainers stood back respectfully and gave them all the time they needed. Diego and Jeremy had talked about this and both boys agreed not to prolong the pain of the moment.

Diego took Aloha to a corner of the lawn and sat down with her. "This is goodbye for now, my sweet girl," he told her as he held her close. "I will pray for you and your success. I'm turning you over to the best trainers you could have. Now it's up to you to make me proud."

Aloha turned her liquid chocolate brown eyes toward his and held his gaze. Diego knew that she understood.

"Aloha, I'll be checking up on you. And I'll come back to your graduation," he promised her. "Goodbye, Aloha. Don't forget me. I love you."

The trainer led her away and Diego walked back toward the car. He could not look back to watch her leave. He didn't see her turn her head as she heard him walk away. He didn't see her wrinkle her nose and send him one last sweet smile.

Chapter Twenty

Don't walk in front of me,
I may not follow.
Don't walk behind me,
I may not lead.
Walk beside me and be my friend.

—Albert Camus

The days dragged by slowly as Diego tried to concentrate more on his life and less on Aloha's. He knew his schoolwork was suffering and struggled to pay attention in the classroom. He thought Jeremy was handling all this better than he was, and wondered what he could do about it. The Guide Dog school was sending the boys monthly updates on the dogs, and they were doing well. The reports made them happy, but still Diego missed Aloha so much.

Walking home from school one day, Diego had an idea.

"Jeremy, let's call Guide Dogs and ask them if we can go see our dogs for a few minutes on Saturday." Diego felt that

Aloha would be comforted by his visit. He was dying to put his arms around her and have her lick his face.

"Hey, you know we can't go. They already told us that." Jeremy searched his friend's face with concern.

"Right, but I thought I'd try. Maybe they would make an exception for us," Diego smiled wistfully. It felt good being courageous enough to say that.

"You know, I think it would be worse for our puppies and us to go see them now. They're in the middle of their training, and we could mess them up."

"Yeah, but I'd give anything to spend ten minutes with Aloha. I miss her so much," Diego confided sadly.

"Me too. Alma was a big part of my life." Jeremy felt the ache in his heart and understood Diego's suffering. This was the first time that either boy had raised a dog, and losing their dogs so quickly was painful.

Suddenly Jeremy had a thought. "Maybe we should apply for another dog. What do you think?"

"Nah, not me. I couldn't replace Aloha. I think it will take me a long time to even want to do this again," responded Diego.

"Yeah, you're right. Let's wait until we've stopped thinking about how hard it was to let them go," added Jeremy, turning off to go to his house. "Bye, see ya tomorrow."

Diego continued down the road. He found himself remembering the day he left Aloha at the school. After handing the leash to the trainer and walking to the car, he remembered falling into the back seat with tears gushing from his eyes. Jeremy's father watched him through the rear-view mirror, brushing away his own tears. Several minutes later Jeremy returned and sat beside Diego. Diego thought of how Jeremy slumped forward, sobbing into his hands. *Even brave, confident boys like Jeremy need their loved ones*, he had thought.

Christmas this year was not nearly as memorable as last year, when they were all exploring St. Augustine, Cocoa Beach, Walt Disney World, and other warm parts of Florida. Diego tried to find cheer and joy in the festivities, but knew his parents worried about his lack of enthusiasm.

One evening in January Diego's cousin from Seattle called him. They had always been close friends growing up, even though she was two years older.

"Hey, Diego, remember that Mexican song we used to sing when we got together? 'Lluvia Fresca' has always been special for us. You still remember it, don't you?" asked Carmen.

"Yeah, I remember it. I told you we could sing it together at your wedding," laughed Diego, remembering the fun times they had shared visiting each other's homes and learning the song in Mexico.

"Good, because I really want you to play it on the piano for me at my 'quinceañera' party in February. You know I'll be fifteen and how important that day is for us! And I want you to be there, along with Aunt Maria Teresa, Uncle Ernesto and Clarita," she coaxed.

"Carmen, I don't have the music to play it on the piano. And there would be so many people there..." Diego was reaching for excuses.

"I have the music and I'll send it to you. Hey, buddy, this means so much to me."

Diego smiled. He knew he wouldn't let her down. Maybe it would even be fun.

Carmen would be having the traditional Latin "*quinceañera*" party to celebrate her transition from child to woman. In the Mexican-American culture, a "*quincenañera*" is a very important milestone in the life of a young girl. Carmen would be "princess" for a day, and her family and relatives would join her in the celebration.

Diego's parents had been asked to be Carmen's "*padrinos*," or godparents. Clara would be a young "*dama*" (attendant) and take part in the ceremony. She would wear an elegant gown and carry flowers. They were all so enthusiastic about this event that it made him feel ashamed to be dwelling on his problems. He learned the piano music and played it proudly for Carmen, who beamed with pleasure.

Carmen was dressed in a lovely pink ball gown with white gloves as she entered St. Mary's Catholic Church for the ceremony. Diego was pleased to see that the mass was spoken in both Spanish and English. Carmen recited her vows unto God and received communion.

Then the fun began. The 150 guests gathered at the community center where the mariachi band welcomed the guests with festive Mexican music. After the presents were opened, the band toned down the songs so that everyone could join in the dancing. Diego danced with his mother and Clara, and then with a lot of pretty girls who were attending. He and his family enjoyed a wonderful dinner and the multi-tiered cake. Later that evening he realized that he had totally forgotten about Aloha for the entire day!

Looking back on the ceremony, Diego agreed that it was beautiful and he was glad he had gone. He and his family spent three days in Seattle, enjoying their relatives and visiting new places.

The day they returned home, Jeremy phoned him with the news.

"Oh my gosh, Diego. I'm so confused. I think it stinks, but I'm not sure..." he muttered.

"What are you talking about, Jeremy?" asked Diego.

"The campus just called me. They said Alma's been dropped. She got to the eighth level, but she couldn't stop growling and alarm barking when people got near her instructor. I guess they tried to counter-condition her, even in the instructor's home, but the behavior continued. They asked me if I would like to pick her up tomorrow. "

Diego didn't know what to say. This was what they both wanted, wasn't it? Now his best friend was going through it and didn't seem to be happy about it.

"Do you want me to come over? I'll jump on the bike and meet you in fifteen minutes," offered Diego.

"Yeah, that would be good."

When Diego arrived, he found Jeremy sitting on the back steps. His eyes were red and he seemed very bewildered.

"I wonder if it's something I did," he said. "They told me that she just started that protective growling stuff but they couldn't correct it, so she has to be career changed. That really sucks. How do you think Alma must feel?"

Diego was surprised at the question. "I think she'll be happy to be back home with you. Aren't you glad, Jeremy?" Diego asked, totally confused at Jeremy's reaction.

"I don't know. I don't know what to feel. I'm sad for her not making it, I feel bad for the blind person, but I'm happy to know she's mine again. What do you think?" Jeremy turned to face Diego for the first time.

"Gee, it's tough knowing that Alma will be back and Aloha might not. I think right now I'm just jealous," grinned Diego. "I always knew you were luckier than me."

The next day Jeremy picked up his dog from Guide Dogs for the Blind. Alma recognized his voice and wriggled with happiness when he called to her. He held on to her for a long moment, so happy she would be his dog for good now.

But he decided to wait for a day before bringing her by to see Diego, not knowing how he would react. He rode his bike to Diego's house with Alma following on the leash. When Diego saw her, he bent over and held her head between his hands.

"How's your sister doing, Alma? Is she thinking about me?" he asked slowly. Then he stood up and softly punched Jeremy's shoulder.

"This is good for us, Jeremy. We have one of them back, and hopefully the other one will do what they were trained to do. Will you share Alma with me?"

Jeremy punched him back and Diego knew the answer to his question.

Chapter Twenty-One

Faith is to believe what we do not see; and the reward of this faith is to see what we believe.

—Saint Augustine

"Nana, how are you going to see to blow out your candles?" asked Tyler skeptically as the cake was brought to their table.

"Well, sweetie, I'll just place my hands above the flames and figure out where they are," answered Kimberly Louise with a sly grin. She did just that and blew out every one of them.

Tyler clapped her little hands with glee. "You are so good, Nana! Can you see again?"

Kimberly Louise thought a moment. "Yes, Tyler, I can see, even if it is with my fingers, my nose and my ears."

"Just like you read with your ears and fingers, right Nana?" asked Jonathan.

"That's right, dear. And thank you again for those wonderful books on tape you gave me for my birthday." She was radiant this evening, and grateful that the birthday dinner had gone so well. She had been blind for more than nine months, and her self-assurance and confidence were evident. Her children and grandchildren had invited her to one of the most elegant restaurants on the island, and she had eaten her dinner without one mishap. They were amazed to watch her navigate her fork around the plate almost as skillfully as a sighted person.

"Nana, I'm putting your cake dish to the right of your coffee at three o'clock." Jonathan enjoyed helping his grandmother by telling her where the food was situated on the plate or table.

Kimberly Louise was proud of her grandchildren and how quickly they adapted to guiding her through social situations. As they got up to leave the table, an acquaintance walked over and extended his hand in greeting. Her grandson quietly told her that he was holding out his hand to shake hers. With her cane in one hand she reached out with the other, holding up her delicate fingers to grasp his and smiling her thanks to Jonathan.

Several days later she jokingly told her family that there should be some form of "in-home training" for family and friends to parallel the training they received in orientation and mobility classes.

"For example," she began, "my friends from school complain that their spouses speak for them in conversations. Thank goodness you don't do that for me!"

"We know better, Mama. You wouldn't stand for that," laughed John Henry.

"Right. Remember that time in the restaurant when the server asked you what Mama wanted to eat and kept referring to Mama as 'she'?" said Julia.

"What happened?" asked Jonathan, his eyes wide in anticipation.

"Oh, my gosh. Well, your elegant grandmother turned toward the server, smiled sweetly and said: 'Young man, 'she' has a name. It's Kimberly Louise. Even though I cannot see you, I can hear you and speak to you. Please do not treat me as if I'm invisible. Kindly do me a favor and acknowledge that I'm present.' Then she left him a huge tip!" giggled Julia.

"Nana, that's a good story!" Tyler loved stories and often asked Kimberly Louise to invent new ones for her. "I'm gonna tell my teacher that one."

"What a great idea, child!" beamed Kimberly Louise, delighted to know that she had played a small part in educating others on how to treat sight-impaired persons. With a wickedly eloquent roll of her eyes she added, "Come on, y'all. Let's go home and I'll tell you some great stories!"

That evening, Kimberly Louise phoned her friend Mimi and planned a day of exercise and swimming for the following morning. She had been thinking about how helpful and loving Mimi was. After both ladies healed from their fractures, Mimi offered to take Kimberly Louise to the gym. They worked with personal trainers, swam after workouts, and were in top physical condition. Kimberly Louise had always exercised, but now she pursued fitness and good health with a personal agenda. She wanted to show others that blind people could do just about anything they wanted to do.

After their workouts, the ladies decided to eat lunch in the Village. They bought some chicken wraps and salads in one of the small cafés and carried them down to the park by the pier. This was just the type of spontaneous activity that Kimberly Louise loved and missed.

"This is terrific, Mimi," she laughed as they ate in the warm sunshine. "We are accompanied by the soft sounds of the ocean waves harmonized by the shrill of seagulls hovering above, waiting to snatch up our crumbs." She listened intently as some blue jays joined the gulls. "Oh, in case you're wondering, I've learned to identify birds by their songs, not by their feathers."

Her friend abruptly turned serious. "Do you see all this in your memory, Kimberly Louise?"

"You know, I have to see this with my imagination, but it comes to me much easier than I thought it would. Maybe I've just developed a better attitude toward my destiny."

"Oh, Kimberly Louise. You've shown a lot of courage

through all of this. I don't think I could have handled it nearly as well." Mimi gave her friend's hand a squeeze.

Kimberly Louise leaned back and stretched her long legs on the bench. "For a while, I wallowed in self-pity. I watched my family suffering because of it, and I prayed for strength. When I finally turned my fear and anger over to the Lord, He took them from me and opened my mind to new opportunities. At that moment, I promised myself to hold the bright jewels of all my good memories close to my heart."

"You've come so far already. But I sense there's a new challenge in that pretty head of yours. What's your next hurdle?" asked Mimi.

"Hmm, you do know me well, dear friend. I've been thinking that it takes one hundred percent of my energy to cope with blindness every moment of every single day. I was wondering if having a guide dog might just take some of the pressure off of me. I like the idea of having another set of eyes. And I could always use the companionship. I'm longing for a true friend, always with me but not seeing me as a burden. Does that sound crazy from a woman who has only had two dogs in her life?"

"The rules of the game have changed for you and you are entitled to start from wherever you want. I've seen you around animals and you love whatever comes your way. I think it's a great idea!" responded Mimi enthusiastically.

"And I guess I'm still searching for that feeling of freedom.

I'm not there yet. Maybe I'll never find it, but I think this might bring me closer. I've done some research and I've found a school in Oregon, near where I went to college, with a fabulous program. We've spoken by phone, and they are willing to come out here to interview me, no strings attached."

"Kimberly Louise, it sounds to me like you've already applied and are ready to go!" exclaimed Mimi.

"Well, sort of. I haven't told my family yet, because I'm not sure I'll go through with it. But I've sent them my tape to show my cane mobility, I have three personal recommendations from doctors and therapists, and I had the physical exam. So I guess I'm more than half way there," she chuckled, her deep blue eyes twinkling.

They sat quietly for a few moments. Suddenly, Kimberly Louise began to speak.

"I had a dream a month or so ago that pushed me into this venture. In the dream, I was searching for freedom, like a bird flying in a large cage. The limited safety of the bird lacks the spark of adventure that the other birds flying high and free have. Then from the top of a mountain I heard a voice calling me, almost pleading to me. Through a haze of clouds, I saw that the voice belonged to me. It was the voice of my own secret longing."

Mimi noticed that her friend's face was filled with emotion, as if all her features were connected to her heart: her eyes, her mouth, even her body language. She understood that this vision was driving her on to new heights, new longings, and new fears. She hugged Kimberly Louise and offered to help in any way to bring this concept to reality.

"Thanks, Mimi. I'll let you know when I decide." She smiled tenderly at her friend. "I have discovered that blindness is a lot like life. It's whatever you make of it."

Chapter Twenty-Two

I don't think of all the misery, but of all the beauty that still remains.

—Anne Frank

Kimberly Louise felt a rush of happiness returning to Oregon. This time she could not see the splendor of the Pacific Northwest, but she truly felt it. Her son had driven her to Guide Dogs for the Blind last night, and already this morning she was thanking the Lord for her good luck. Her assigned roommate at the Guide Dogs for the Blind School was a wonderfully bright and witty middle-aged lady from Idaho named Barbie, who had been blind for four years. Like Kimberly Louise, she was training for a guide dog because she longed for more freedom and independence in her life.

"I kept imagining something better for me out there, and just hoped I had the persistence and will to make it happen. You know, I think I'm searching for some joy. Maybe my dog will bring that back into my life," explained Barbie as they discussed their excitement over this big change in their lives.

"Well, I'm just grateful that my roommate has the same sense of order that I have, since our only privacy is the closet between our beds," joked Kimberly Louise. "That's the one constraint of blindness that actually suits me. I do love order!"

Barbie and Kimberly Louise had a great deal in common. Each one had two grown children whom they adored. Both women were physically fit, frank and outspoken, and each one had challenged the conventions of their times. They discovered that they both felt blessed by good fortune in life, despite their disability. They roared with laughter when they shared their common lifetime pursuit of "wanting it all," and their constant search to obtain it. Now they realized they were closer to reaching their goal than before they lost their sight.

"You know, Barbie, blindness turned me from an adult back to a child. I depended on my family for everything. I hated that dependency and fought it for quite a time, finally accepting it. Talk about a humbling experience!" Kimberly Louise shuddered at the thought.

Their program was four weeks long and the days were packed with classroom lectures and hands-on training. There were twelve students in attendance for this class. They began with lectures on Orientation, Introduction to the Guide Dog, and Communication with the Guide Dog.

The instructor presented the "point of view of the dog."

"Consider that the puppies were separated at eight weeks from their mother and siblings and given to raisers, where they lived happily for a year to a year and a half. They were then returned to the training school where they will be in training anywhere from four months to a year. During the training period they establish a loving relationship with the staff, only to be separated from them and placed with their blind partner," Susi explained. She was one of four instructors who was working with this class.

The students soon began to understand how important this partnership of dog and master would become.

"In many ways, the relationship between the guide dog and blind owner is like courtship and marriage. There is the coming together, the careful getting to know each other, and the joy and excitement of early love. Then gradually, that excitement turns into a comfortable warm belonging. Each learns what the other wants and needs, and what he is going to do." Susi had a warm and gentle voice, soothing to both the students and the canines.

She continued. "Guide dog training is a seamless process in which a dog progresses at its own pace, slowly transitioning from one phase to the other. There are ten phases in the dogs' training, usually two to three weeks in length. Most of the dogs are in training four to five months, but some stay in training for nine months or more, waiting to be matched up with just the perfect partner."

Kimberly Louise began to daydream about her dog. She knew that Guide Dogs for the Blind individually matched each student with the appropriate dog for their needs. In fact, the students didn't arrive at the school until at least two dogs were pre-selected for them. The selection was based on their activities, life styles, personalities and many other factors. What would her dog be like? She smiled to herself.

"So, during these four weeks you will be taught and then you'll put into practice everything the dog has learned in these ten phases of training. The first three days you will work without your dogs. Your instructors will be your 'dog,' who we call 'Juno.' We'll hold the chest part of the harness; you'll hold the handle and give us the commands. You will learn that every command has a verbal sound, footwork and body gestures, which the dogs already know. We'll start out in peaceful surroundings and end up in traffic. Then, on Wednesday, you'll receive your dog and we'll do it all over again with your new partner."

The room became quiet as each student reflected on Susi's words.

Will my dog like me? thought Kimberly Louise. Other students had the same question.

As if reading their minds, Susi continued. "It will probably take six to eight days for your dog to know you and bond with you. Remember, the dogs may be reluctant to replace the deep bond they've now made with their instructors. For that reason, they haven't worked with or even been around the instructors for several days before you get them."

"Think about this: the day you receive them each of you will be entering this relationship as individuals and emerging as a team."

The students silently absorbed this information. Susi did not tell them that the instructors also suffered the change, that they felt the loss the day they matched the dogs with the students. These instructors loved the dogs they trained, just as the raisers before them loved them. It was a continual circle of joy and pain and sadness. The reward was in seeing the students put all their trust in the dogs, and the dogs responding to them by taking the responsibility. That gave the instructors a deep sense of accomplishment and pride.

"As you know, class, once you receive your dog, he or she will live with you in your room for the remainder of the course. We'll do our initial training on the campus and then move out to various locations, starting with rural areas, then small towns, and finally, we'll go to Portland. Your days will then begin at 6 a.m. when you take your dogs out for relief before breakfast. Sundays are free and visitors are allowed in the afternoon."

As Kimberly Louise and Barbie walked back to their room, they commented on everything they had learned.

"I guess we'll not be using our white canes much anymore," said Kimberly Louise.

"Oh, but the dogs will be so much better. I feel like a kid ready to enter Disneyland! Isn't it great to feel such happiness again?" asked Barbie.

They walked into their room and heard the soft patter of the rain against their window. Kimberly Louise smiled and linked her arm through Barbie's.

"Can you hear the lovely lullaby of the rain? It's a subtle, fragile concept that we might have missed before we became sight-impaired. That's another bonus to blindness: listening more attentively. I'm learning to focus on and trust my hearing."

Barbie walked to her bed and brought Kimberly Louise a quilt.

"My daughter and her girlfriends made this for me shortly after I lost my sight. It's made of fabrics of my life, scenes of places I love, pictures of the faces I adore. Even though I can't see them, I can feel them and their colors and textures add strength to my heart. Gaze at it with your hands. I call this tapestry of interwoven threads 'Independence.' Our dogs will take us there."

Chapter Twenty-Three

We know what we are, but know not what we may be.

—William Shakespeare

"It felt so good to be showing those high school kids something new," smiled Diego as he and Jeremy finished up their presentation with Alma.

"Yeah, and they were really interested in the Puppy Raising Program. We got so many questions from the students! And the faculty too!" Jeremy seemed delighted with the student body response to their Outreach Program.

Diego, Jeremy and Alma had just returned from presenting their program to Grant High School in Portland. They were excited and enthusiastic after a successful reception from the school.

Maria Teresa dropped Jeremy and Alma off at his house, and then drove the three miles to their house. She had enjoyed watching the boys and Alma educating the high school students about raising dogs for the blind.

"Diego, I'm so proud of what you are doing in the community," she told her son as she sat across from him at the table.

"Thanks, Mamá," he replied. "It just makes me happy that I can speak intelligently about something we all know so well."

Diego went upstairs to his room and flopped down on the bed. Closing his eyes, he found himself re-living the unfolding of recent events.

At the end of his seventh grade school year, his English teacher had entered Diego's essay, "Giving Back to the Community," in a statewide contest. To his surprise and pleasure, Diego won second place. He was awarded $500 and was quickly afforded many opportunities to educate others about his passion. The state newspaper wrote an article about him and the local television station did an interview. Through it all, Diego presented himself with poise and confidence. Then the schools in the area called to ask him to speak about the Puppy Raising Program.

Diego conferred with Jeremy.

"Jeremy, would you and Alma form a team with me to go out and speak to the schools? I don't want to do this alone, and it would be so much better if we could take Alma and demonstrate what our dogs can do."

Jeremy smiled at his friend. "Sure, I'll go. Do you think we can work it out at our school?"

Their principal, Mr. Johnson, proposed this venture to the faculty, who readily agreed to give the boys time to do this Outreach Program. They allowed Diego and Jeremy two afternoons a month to visit Portland area schools.

The boys set up their presentation. Diego was the main speaker. He explained the process of raising a dog for the blind. Jeremy then introduced Alma and explained the commands she would demonstrate. Alma walked through her routine, the audience was thrilled and the students were given an opportunity to ask questions. Both Jeremy and Diego answered the many questions and Alma was rewarded with pats and hugs.

It seemed that Jeremy and Diego had grown even closer through these presentations. Diego knew that Jeremy cooperated in part to ease Diego's pain for giving up Aloha. Jeremy knew that Diego included him because of their strong bonding through their dogs. The three of them made a fantastic team, and their presentation was booked in schools for months in advance.

When Diego opened his eyes, he realized that he'd fallen asleep. He had been dreaming about Aloha. They were running recklessly together in red poppy fields. She was not on a leash, but running freely and happily. Diego was trying to catch her, his arms above his head and his smile wide and joyful. When Aloha finally stopped and lay panting on the flowers, Diego threw himself across her back.

"Aloha, you are my *muchachita*. I love you, my girl. You make me so happy." He hugged her hard.

His dream ended abruptly. He shook his head and searched his mind for clarity. She was in training, an hour away, becoming the guide dog she was destined to be. Some very lucky person would get to live out Aloha's days with her. But Diego had the awesome responsibility and the good fortune to have prepared her for this goal. The dream brought it all into perspective.

"Good girl, Aloha." Diego spoke softly and tenderly. "I know now that you are going to make it."

Chapter Twenty-Four

And my God will meet all your needs according to His glorious riches in Christ Jesus.

—Philippians 4:19

"Here on campus, in approximately five to eight months, give or take, your dog has learned to lead a person from point to point in a straight line, to stop for all changes in elevation, such as curbs and stairs, and to avoid obstacles in the path. The puppy raisers and the trainers have also taught the dogs to ignore distractions while working. But the guide dog will not relieve you of making decisions and using common sense." Peter was instructing the class today and preparing them for meeting their dogs this afternoon.

"However, there is a concept called 'intelligent disobedience,' which I consider to be the dog's most important job. We teach the dogs to disobey commands when the situation is unsafe. But protecting you seems to be inherent in them. We believe it's based on the love your dog has for you."

He continued. "Morris Frank was the first guide dog user in America. He told his dog Buddy to walk into an elevator. Buddy refused. Morris had heard the elevator doors open, so he repeated the command. 'Buddy, forward,' he said. Buddy didn't move. In frustration, Morris stepped toward the elevator. Buddy threw himself across his feet, preventing any forward movement. The elevator shaft was empty. Buddy saved his partner from falling to his death."

The class buzzed with amazement.

"One of the dogs from our school had the self-confidence to disobey his blind owner when she unknowingly ordered him to step into a flooded street. He saved her from trauma and possible injury."

"Then there's the story of Michael Hingson, who worked on the 78th floor of the World Trade Center in New York City. On September 11, 2001, after the plane hit the building eighteen floors above him, he felt for his yellow Lab guide, 'Roselle,' who was sleeping at his feet. The building was shaking, the air filled with smoke, fire, and the smell of jet fuel. He commanded Roselle to go forward and she led him through the disheveled office to the stairwell and down the long descent. When they reached the bottom, breathing became almost impossible. Roselle was panting and wanted to drink the water that was pooled on the floor. But they had to leave the building quickly. They were two blocks away when Tower 2 collapsed. They ran stumbling toward the subway, which was no longer operational. The entire time Roselle remained focused on her work."

Peter took a deep breath. "Then Tower 1 toppled, showering them with ash and debris. Roselle guided Michael to the home of a friend in mid-Manhattan where they stayed until the trains were running again. That, people, is an example of what your guide dog can do for you."

No one spoke. The room was silent.

"If you make a mistake in judgment and try to cross the street at the wrong time, the guide dog won't cross. He will come to a dead halt if crossing it would put you in danger," added Susi. "This is what they've been trained to do with all the exercises before you meet them. Through early 'pattern training' we've cued correct guide work responses with shaping and positive reinforcement. As the dogs gain confidence, they take the initiative to problem solve travel challenges. Eventually they will use 'intelligent disobedience' when necessary, disobeying any command that would put the team in danger."

As they listened to everything the dogs had to learn to do in order to protect and guide them, the students felt an overwhelming appreciation for these marvelous companions. They realized that the dogs would enable them to go places they could not otherwise go.

Later that afternoon, the instructors took them aside and spoke to them about their dogs. Kimberly Louise was told that her dog would be a female yellow Lab named Aloha. Her roommate was getting a female Golden Retriever called Jada. They returned to their rooms, waiting to be called into the instructors' office to meet their dogs.

"Barbie, you know we shouldn't pet each other's dogs for a few days so that our dog will realize that she's ours alone. That will be hard for me to do," confided Kimberly Louise to her roommate.

Barbie returned first with Jada on the leash and sat on her bed, cupping the lovely dog's face in her hands. Jada seemed to respond to her voice, slowly wagging her tail and finally settling at her feet.

The instructor called Kimberly Louise into the office. She instantly felt the presence of Aloha. She softly called her name, and Aloha thumped her tail and walked toward her. Kimberly Louise was flooded with love.

"Aloha, good girl," she cooed lovingly. She squatted down to her level and touched her smooth head, patting her gently. After several seconds, Aloha stretched, lay down and rolled over on her back.

"Where did she go?" asked Kimberly Louise worriedly.

"She's right in front of you with her feet in the air and tummy upturned, waiting for you to rub her belly," laughed Peter.

Kimberly Louise obliged with a giggle, and then took the

leash and led her to their room. "Aloha, heel," she gently commanded. She walked the short distance from the office to her room with a dancing heart and an enormous smile.

Chapter Twenty-Five

The hilltop hour would not be half so wonderful
if there were no dark valley to traverse.

—Hellen Keller

It was Saturday afternoon and they had been walking a long route through the streets of Gresham, Oregon. Aloha was leading Kimberly Louise around obstacles on the streets and sidewalks, hesitating at every street corner or raised surface. She stopped suddenly when she saw a car rapidly approaching, even though Kimberly Louise had urged her forward.

"Good girl," praised Kimberly Louise, petting her head and rubbing her ears. "Aloha is my wonderful smart girl."

"Aloha, forward," she continued, surprised at the assurance in her voice.

They had been working together almost two weeks now and had formed a tremendous bond. She felt that Aloha trusted her and loved being with her. She knew she felt the same about Aloha. All these thoughts were whirling in her mind as they headed back to the van.

"You just passed a cat," Peter told her, with pride in his voice. "Aloha didn't even look at it, just as she's been trained."

Suddenly it happened. That spark of love pierced her heart. She had known that guide dogs were trained to ignore everything but the safety of their partners, that they give up a great part of their doggy lives for their owners. But now she saw it differently. This was not just a guide dog; this was her Aloha, and she was doing this for her. Aloha was her dog and she was Aloha's human.

Thank you, she spoke silently. *Thank you, God. I'm free. I'm finally complete.*

The next morning the instructors told her she had visitors. She wasn't expecting anyone, and was surprised and cautious. She put on Aloha's harness and they walked to the visitor's lounge.

"Nana, what a pretty dog you have!" whooped Tyler as she threw herself into her grandmother's arms.

"Tyler, what a glorious surprise!" laughed Kimberly Louise. "Where's Jonathan and your parents?"

"Right here, Mama. We're all here. Donald too," answered Julia, pulling her husband forward. "You knew we couldn't come to your graduation, but we wanted to surprise you this weekend. I see that we did." She ran to her mother and held her in a long embrace.

Kimberly Louise was overcome with joy, and let the tears flow freely from her eyes. What wonderful children she had! Her son John Henry was coming for her graduation, and her daughter and family were here today.

"Nana, we flew all the way across the United States to be the first to meet Aloha," bragged Jonathan. "It was so cool! Aloha is looking at us like she likes us already. Can I pet her?"

They spent the morning touring the campus and catching up. Then Kimberly Louise accompanied them on a long drive, listening with interest as they described the beauty of the cedars and Douglas fir trees with the backdrop of the mountains. Aloha stayed on campus and was exercised by the staff during their absence.

Her family took her to an elegant restaurant for lunch, recommended by her instructor Susi. Their afternoon was spent in delightful fellowship, and was ending much too quickly.

"Nana, tell me a story about Aloha," begged Tyler. "Do you ever dream about her?"

"It's funny you should ask me that, Tyler. Two nights ago I dreamed that I could see. Aloha ran free in my dream, and we played and romped together. It was so much fun."

"Do you dream in color?" asked Jonathan.

"Yes, almost always. But often I'm blind in my dreams, yet still watching everything that happens. How unusual. I guess

I have lots of memories to draw on. Plus my ability to imagine has intensified, and it is there that the blind can outshine the seeing." She smiled at her grandson, feeling that he understood.

"Well, we should get you back to the campus. Your curfew is almost here," said Donald after a moment. No one wanted to get up.

"Mama, we'll see you again in less than two weeks. We'll have your house all fixed up and ready for Aloha's arrival, and after you rest a day, we're going to throw you a big party!" Julia was so proud of her mother and the progress she'd made. She thought she had never looked so full of life.

The following week Kimberly Louise was given Diego Escobár's phone number. All of the students called their dog raisers to introduce themselves, and some of them invited them for dinner the night before graduation.

"Hello Diego. I'm Kimberly Louise Walker and I've been the fortunate lady to receive Aloha. I'd like to invite you and your family to dinner Friday night to thank you for all your love and effort you put into raising her."

Diego felt so excited. He'd been waiting all these months to find out who Aloha would be placed with, and now he would meet her!

"I'll put my parents on the phone," was all he could manage to say.

Diego's parents thanked her for the invitation, and then

explained that they felt that only Diego should go, giving him the opportunity to get to know her and learn about Aloha's progress.

On the evening before graduation, they drove him to the designated restaurant in Gresham, a small town close to Boring. After meeting Kimberly Louise and thanking her for her kindness to their son, they agreed on a time to pick him up at the restaurant at the end of the evening.

Diego could hardly wait to start asking questions about Aloha. As soon as they were seated, he initiated the conversation.

"Mrs. Walker, I'm so excited to hear anything about Aloha. Could you please tell me everything she is doing," began Diego, running his words together in his excitement to hear about his sweet Aloha.

Kimberly Louise threw back her head and laughed. "Diego, please call me Miss Kimberly Louise. You are right. I do have so much to tell you. Let's get started."

They talked all through the meal. After they exhausted the topic of Aloha, they discovered that both of them were computer nuts. That gave them fodder for conversation long after dessert was finished.

"I see that we're going to be good friends, Diego. What a pleasure it is for me to meet the person who raised Aloha so successfully. Tomorrow we shall plan your first visit to Georgia."

Chapter Twenty-Six

Kindness gives birth to kindness.

—Sophocles

Diego and the other raisers were sitting in a side room next to the auditorium. As their names were called, they walked their dogs up the steps to the stage, and presented them to their new partners. They could hear the speeches from their little room, but Diego was not really listening. He was rubbing Aloha's ears, scratching her tummy and just enjoying having this time with her.

He arrived at Guide Dogs for the Blind several hours earlier with his parents, Clara and Jeremy for their reunion with Aloha. The night before he and Kimberly Louise had met for dinner, but she could not take Aloha. This morning was the first time he would see her in almost seven months!

What a happy reunion it was! Kimberly Louise was waiting in the lounge when they arrived. When Aloha saw them coming, her movements quickened with excitement and her tail wagged so hard that her body trembled. She reached

Diego and nudged him with her wet nose, overcome with love and happiness. Kimberly Louise offered Diego the leash and stepped back, allowing him his time with his dog.

When he leaned down to hug her, she rolled on the floor in her tummy scratching position. Susi was watching from a distance and laughed out loud.

"So that's where Aloha learned this trick," she teased as she approached them. "She sure kept me busy rubbing that tummy."

As Diego held her and played with her, Aloha made a contented purring noise deep in her throat. After a time she got up and greeted all her loved ones, offering each one her tummy for rubbing and her ears for stroking. Aloha was wriggling with delight at all the attention.

Kimberly Louise's son, John Henry, was waiting for them in her dormitory room. He was a handsome and affable young man who clearly adored his mother. The two families spent the rest of the morning together and found that they enjoyed each other's company. Diego and his family liked Kimberly Louise's dry sense of humor and admired her poise and charm. Jeremy loved her southern accent. Clara was infatuated with her beauty.

"Miss Kimberly Louise, you have such beautiful hair. Has it always been long and red and wavy?" she asked.

"Why yes, precious, it has," answered Kimberly Louise. "Let me feel your hair." As she touched Clara's medium length curly hair, she took out her brush from the drawer. "Shall we brush each other's hair? I'm pretty good at fancy hairdos."

After a few moments, Clara had a swept-up chignon, with French braids accenting the sides. She took the mirror and was amazed at what she saw.

"Wow! I look grown-up. This is so cool." She took Kimberly Louise by the hand and sat her down."Now I want to put some ribbons in your hair, to match your dress."

Kimberly Louise had gathered her hair into a sleek low ponytail. It looked quite chic and sophisticated. Clara pulled red and yellow ribbons from her backpack and asked Miss Kimberly Louise if she could put them in her hair. Kimberly Louise readily agreed and soon she was decorated and laughing with glee.

"How do I look, John Henry? Can you recognize your Mama with all this fanciness?"

"You look lovely. I've never seen you prettier." John Henry realized he'd not seen her this happy since before the accident.

"Let's go to the ceremony like this," beamed Clara. "We look like we belong together."

"Yes, we do. I want you to come to Georgia and meet my grandchildren. I have one who is just your age," said Kimberly Louise, hugging Clara closely.

Maria Teresa and Ernesto exchanged smiles. They were

pleased to see that Aloha's new owner was such a delightful person. She was entertaining Diego to keep his mind from dwelling on the afternoon ceremony, and being a gracious hostess to all of them as well. The morning passed by quickly.

After a light snack, they separated and the family members went into the auditorium and found their places. Diego and the other raisers were given their dogs and asked to wait in the adjoining room until their names were called. Jeremy was allowed to stay with Diego, and Diego was grateful for that.

His best friend had been very supportive after Diego received the phone call to tell him that Aloha would be graduating in two weeks.

"Well, it's a done deal. She made it." He broke the news to Jeremy as they walked through the woods with Alma the afternoon of the call.

Jeremy stopped in his tracks. He looked closely at Diego, and then reached out to hug him.

"Congratulations, Diego. We passed one and kept one," he told him with uncertainty.

Diego chuckled and slapped his friend on the back. "You got that right. Way to go, Aloha!"

He shifted his thoughts back to the present. He looked out the window and discovered what a beautiful spring day it was. The sun was shining with warm air blowing through the treetops: a celebratory day to escort Aloha into the rest of her life. He suddenly realized he was listening to the clear voice of another puppy raiser presenting her dog to the graduate.

"It's been a big payoff. I'm really proud of her," she was telling the audience. She handed the leash to the graduating student.

"I know you will love her like I do and know that wherever you go, you'll walk with a piece of my heart beside you."

He looked down at Aloha lying peacefully at his feet. *A piece of my heart beside you*, he thought. *That's what I'm sending away with you, my muchachita.*

Now I can really let you go.

Chapter Twenty-Seven

If I can ease one life the aching,
or cool one pain . . .
I shall not live in vain.

—Emily Dickinson

Kimberly Louise was seated on the stage with her eleven classmates. She was listening closely to the speeches and wondering what she would say when her time came. She hadn't prepared a speech and was simply enjoying the ceremony. The Executive Director had spoken and was followed by the lead instructor, who shared the process of educating the dogs and students, and finally, the dog-student team.

Her classmates ranged in age from twenty-three to seventy-five years old. Before the presentation of the dogs began, she and the others had given their instructors a beautifully painted board with each one's left hand print, symbolizing the hand they used to guide the dog. Each print was painted the color of the student's dog, with both names written inside by the graduate. Most of their dogs were white or yellow so there were eleven yellow and white hand prints. But since one student had received a black Lab named Nathaniel, there was also one black hand print. The end result was beautiful, with dog paws surrounding the prints. At the conclusion of this presentation, the instructors and audience were moved to tears.

Kimberly Louise listened as her dear friend Barbie was thanking her raiser, their dog standing proudly between them.

"These dogs are so much better than walking around with a big white stick," Barbie joked. "And with Jada, I know I'm safe. I know she wants to be with me. I just can't describe to you what it means to have a pair of eyes. Thank you, Karen, for preparing her for me and giving me the best angel in the world."

Her puppy raiser leaned over to give her a hug. Tears filled her eyes, but she managed to find her voice.

"We can give our children two things: roots and wings. We also teach our puppies roots; then they come here and get more roots. And when they are finally ready to go to their owners, they get their wings. Your little angel Jada now has hers."

Kimberly Louise wiped the tears from her eyes as she heard Diego's name being called. She was helped to the podium where she found Diego waiting for her. He took her hand in his and placed the leash in her palm. Aloha wagged her tail happily as she sat down between them.

Kimberly Louise stood tall with her arm around Diego's shoulders and spoke warmly.

"Thank you, Guide Dogs for the Blind, for presenting me with two marvelous new friends. Aloha has given me back my freedom and independence, and Diego has given me a gift of sight as precious as the gift of physical sight." She turned to face Diego, taking both of his hands in hers.

"Diego, by selflessly loving and preparing Aloha for me, you have rekindled the spark that went out of my life when I lost my sight. Now Aloha has found two masters to love. She and I will be waiting for you and your family in our home in Georgia." She reached for his shoulders and wrapped him in a hug.

As Diego began to speak, he searched for his family. Clara's eyes were radiant, and she was beaming with pride for everything he had done. She sent him a tiny wave and blew him a kiss. He returned her smile and realized he was no longer nervous, but suddenly relaxed.

"The other day I was thinking about the parents of President Lincoln. They must have known when they were raising him that he would grow up to be great. When I first saw Aloha, I knew she would be totally awesome. My family and I have raised her to be a hero for Miss Kimberly Louise."

"This is a real tough day for me. It's so hard to let her go far away from my life. All through the training, they kept telling us that raising the puppies is a gift of service to others. But I also think it's also a gift of love to ourselves. We'll have a part of our puppies in our hearts forever."

"This morning, when I saw Aloha lay her head on Miss Kimberly Louise's knee, at first I felt really weird and emotional, and even a little jealous. And then I saw their powerful connection. That was the moment when I knew that losing her was worthwhile, because she now is where she was always meant to be."

Diego didn't hear the resounding applause that followed his speech. He concentrated on leading Kimberly Louise to her chair, where he stood behind her and listened to the last two presentations. These were followed by the guide dog demonstration, which concluded the ceremony. Snacks and refreshments were served and the guests were encouraged to mingle with the graduates, instructors, raisers and especially the dogs.

A couple approached Diego and his family, smiling broadly.

"Hi, we're Rosalie and George Anderson." The gentleman introduced himself and his wife. "Our dog Maggie birthed Aloha and Aztec and we flew up here to see them graduate."

Diego's eyes opened wide. "Wow! You came from San Rafael to see our dogs graduate?" He was amazed.

"Yes, and I'm so happy to see how well they've done," smiled Rosalie. "Congratulations to all of you!"

George turned to Jeremy, standing off to the side. "I understand you are the proud owner and raiser of Alma, who our dog Maggie also birthed. You are a lucky guy to have that special girl. She brought us a lot of joy."

Jeremy beamed. "Yes, she's a wonderful dog. It's so nice to meet you," he added shyly.

On the other side of the room, Wendy was proudly announcing to anyone interested that she would be picking up her new puppy in a few days. Diego and Jeremy exchanged secret smiles and rolled their eyes whenever she approached their group.

Diego knew his family must be tired by now. He was ready to go home. He and Kimberly Louise had already exchanged phone numbers and e-mail addresses. She again invited them to visit her in the fall. To Diego's great delight, his parents had already promised them they would seriously consider it. They talked about meeting in Savannah, Georgia and then driving to Kimberly Louise's home on St. Simons Island.

"Papá, today wasn't as hard as I thought," confided Diego to his father as they stood outside together. "Thanks for all the encouragement you gave me during these months." He smiled his appreciation.

"*Hijo mío*, helping you raise Aloha has been one of the

greatest gifts I've ever received," said Ernesto, sliding his arm around him. "Thank you for that."

This time saying goodbye to Aloha was less painful than before. As they were leaving, Diego remembered he had one more surprise to share with Kimberly Louise.

"Miss Kimberly Louise, do you know what her name means in Hawaiian?" he asked with a smile.

"Why yes, Diego, I think so. Doesn't it mean 'Hello'?"

"That's part of it, but it means so much more. It means 'Hello, Goodbye, I love you.' Isn't that just perfect for our sweet girl?"

"Yes, it's perfect," she looked pleased. "And now I can say 'Aloha' to you and mean it with all my heart."

Hearing her name, Aloha wrinkled her nose in a smile, thumped her tail and rolled onto her back, telling her partner she was ready for her tummy rub.

Resources

PRINTED WORD

The following books were invaluable in my research. They will be helpful to young readers and adults alike.

Do You Remember the Color Blue?, Sally Hobart Alexander, Viking Press. 2000

Friendship in the Dark, Phyllis Campbell, Brett Books, Inc. 1996

Second Sight, Robert V. Hine, The Regents of the University of California. 1993

Seeing in Special Ways, Thomas Bergman, Gareth Stevens Children's Books. 1989

So That Others May Live, Caroline Hebard, Bantam Books. 1995

Twilight, Losing Sight, Gaining Insight, Henry Grunwald, Alfred A. Knopf. 2000

What Blind People Wish Sighted People Knew About Blindness, Harry Martin, AE Press. 1996

ORGANIZATIONS

Guide Dogs for the Blind

350 Los Ranchitos Road, San Rafael, CA 94903
32901 S.E. Kelso Road, Boring, OR 97009
(800) 295-4050

Lions Club International

300 w. 22nd Street, Oak Brook, IL 63523-8842
(630) 572-5466

Georgia Lions's Camp for the Blind
5626 Laura Walker Road, Waycross, GA 31503
(912) 283-4320

Roosevelt Warm Springs Institute for Rehabilitation
P.O. Box 1000, Warm Springs, GA 31830-0268
(706) 655-5000

INTERVIEWS

Cary Leach, Public Affairs Officer, Guide Dogs for the Blind, Boring, OR

Taryn Asbell, Counselor for Georgia Lions Camp for the Blind, Waycross, GA

Christopher Bachelor, Counselor for Georgia Lions Camp for the Blind, Waycross, GA

Demartá Homer, Counselor for Georgia Lions Camp for the Blind, Waycross, GA

Travis Parks, Counselor for Georgia Lions Camp for the Blind, Waycross, GA

Ticiana and Ted Gordillo, Puppy Raisers for Guide Dogs for the Blind, Beaverton, OR

Brandon Jones, Puppy Raiser for Guide Dogs for the Blind, Seattle, WA

Jim Pettigrew, sight-impaired author, St. Simons Island, GA

Manny Zapata, Counselor for Savannah Association for the Blind, Savannah, GA

ADDITIONAL GUIDE DOG SCHOOLS

Eye Dog Foundations for the Blind, Inc.
211 s. Montclair Street
Bakersfield, CA 93309
(800) 393-3641

Eye of the Pacific Guide Dog and Mobility Services, Inc.
747 Amana St. #407
Honolulu, HI 96814
(808) 941-1088

Fidelco Guide Dog Foundation
P.O. Box 142
Bloomfield, CT 06002
(860) 243-5200

Guide Dogs of America International Guiding Eye Program
13445 Glen Oaks Blvd.
Sylmar, CA 91342
(818) 362-5834

Guide Dogs of the Desert
P.O. Box 1692
Palm Springs, CA 92263
(619) 329-6257

Guiding Eyes for the Blind, Inc.
611 Granite Springs Rd.
Yorktown Heights, NY 10598
(800) 942-0149

Guide Dog Foundation for the Blind, Inc
371 E. Jericho Turnpike
Smithtown, NY 11787-2976
(800) 548-4337

Leader Dogs for the Blind
Rochester, MI 48307-3115
(888) 777-5332

Pilot Dogs, Inc.
625 West Town St.
Columbus, OH 43215
(614) 221-6367

The Seeing Eye, Inc.
P.O. Box 375
Morristown, NJ 07963-0375
(973) 539-4425

Southeastern Guide Dogs, Inc.
4210 77th St. East
Palmetto, FL 34221
(800) 944-3647

CANADA

Lions Foundation of Canada Canine Vision Canada
P.O. Box 907, Oakville, Ontario, Canada L6J 5E8
(800) 768-3030

About the Author

Pamela Bauer Mueller was raised in Oregon and graduated from Lewis and Clark College in Portland, Oregon. She worked as a flight attendant for Pan American Airlines before moving to Mexico City, where she lived for eighteen years. Pamela is bicultural as well as bilingual. She has worked as a commercial model, actress, and an English and Spanish language instructor during her years in Mexico. After returning to the United States, Pamela worked for twelve years as a U.S. Customs inspector. After serving six years in San Diego, California, she was selected to work a foreign assignment in Vancouver, British Columbia, Canada. Pamela took an early retirement from U.S. Customs to follow her husband, Michael, who received an instructor position at the Federal Law Enforcement Training Center in Brunswick, Georgia. They reside on St. Simons Island, Georgia with their cats, Jasper and Emmeline. Pamela completed *The Kiska Trilogy* and *Hello, Goodbye, I Love You* in Georgia, and now looks forward to writing historical novels in her new southern home.